# UNHOLY
# REVENGE

## DONALIE BELTRAN

UNHOLY REVENGE
Copyright © 2018 Donalie Beltran

ISBN-10:  0-9896362-8-3
ISBN-13:  978-0-9896362-8-5

Available in paperback and eBook

Published by:  Killing Time Press, LLC

# DEDICATION

This book is dedicated to the wonderful people who buy my books and love my writing – You.

Without you, there would never be books, fiction or non-fiction, flowing out of me. I love writing and am always amazed you still love the results!

Thank you for your patience and support as I continue my best to entertain you.

# ACKNOWLEDGMENTS

I would like to thank Police Departments, all across our country, for their service and the sacrifices they continually make to keep us safe. Although it may not seem like it at times, most of the people you protect are very grateful.

My special thanks to the Wichita P.D. You guys are amazing. Keep up the good work!

My family and I have the utmost respect for what police officers do and the dangers they face every day. Our prayers go with you.

God bless you all.

# CONTENTS

# UNHOLY
# REVENGE

# Chapter 1

"MCGREGOR, DECKER! IN MY OFFICE!"

Detective Donna Decker shot a worried glance across the desk facing hers, to her partner, Lou McGregor. When Chief Parry yells for you, it is never good.

Both jumped up and headed toward the office of the Chief of the Homicide Division. They didn't bother acknowledging the sympathy looks from co-workers. Every Detective in that department has been in their shoes before.

What started out to be a quiet Thursday, wasn't going to end that way.

Upon arriving Donna shut the office door, and both sat down in front of Parry's desk. The Boss would get cranky if McGregor stood. Lou is six-foot-two, so a sitting Parry would have to crane his neck to talk to him.

"Playtime is over, children. Here is your next case. Apparently a severed head has been found in a swimming pool in Vickridge. Now before you go thinking this is just another fun time on the job, it appears to be the eighteen-year-old daughter of Judge Gattino!"

Both detectives inhaled sharply and glanced at each other. Severed heads didn't happen often in Wichita, and few things could be worse to deal with. Then top it off as belonging to a popular, well-known family like the Gattino's, the media is going to have a hay day. That always makes their job more difficult. Not impossible, but difficult.

The media doesn't seem to understand the constant harassment for information about a case just slows things down. Yes, the public has a right to know if there is a killer among them, but they are consistently the first to know when someone is apprehended.

There was always information that couldn't be released, of course. You don't want to tip off the guilty parties before they are apprehended.

Donna loved her job as a detective and enjoyed working with her light-skinned African American partner. At five-foot-seven in three inch-heeled boots, she was a little intimidated by his tall stature, but his remarkable good looks made up for it. She was, however, a bit shocked at their new assignment.

The Chief slammed a folder down in front of them and yelled, "WELL, GET ON IT! It's not nap time around here, you know!"

Donna grabbed the folder as they both jumped up. They left Parry's office to grab their gear. Neither detective blamed him for his attitude. They knew the Chief was a friend of Judge Gattino. It doesn't get more personal than that.

"As usual, I will drive while you let me know what we have," Lou said. They left in his Mercedes.

"Seems the call came from a neighbor who saw the head floating from her second-floor window. Man, that would wake you up in the morning!" Donna's distressed look was not lost on Lou.

"I can't imagine what the Judge is going through right now." Lou has met the judge and admired him. Judge Gattino knew most of the homicide detectives by name since a lot of them had testified in his court over the years. Lou was no exception.

"No one has told him. He is on the bench today and his wife, Gracie, is in Kansas City visiting her mother this week," Donna kept reading. "Lou, I hope this doesn't mean we will be the ones that will have to inform him." If she didn't love being a detective, things like this would turn her sour to the job.

"What did the woman say? The head was a female?" Lou preferred to drive. It gave him a chance to think about the information provided to him by his partner.

"Yep. It says here she thinks it is the eighteen-year-old girl who lives there. It seems the hair color, etc. is the same. Hang on tight, partner, cause this one could get really ugly."

"Why? What is different about this murder over any other?" Lou did not register her concern.

"As you know, we are headed to the high-end area of Vickridge. And even the 'low' end is expensive. The address is for Judge Barton

Albert Gattino. Because he is so well known, the media will probably beat us there!"

"Gattino is a good judge," Lou was talking to himself as much as Donna. "Strict, but fair. So you think it is his child?"

"I have no idea, but if it is, this will make headlines for weeks. That will put a lot more pressure on us to solve it."

Just as they pulled into Vickridge, they could see the police squads lining part of the first block.

Lou parked his car, and they walked towards the gate going into the backyard of the Judge's house. They could see Officer Bowler standing in wait.

What really surprised them was the TV media truck that had been parked at the curb was now pulling away from the house and leaving.

"There is no need to panic, guys. No one died here. The head is a mannequin!" Bowler had to chuckle.

"You are *kidding* me!" Donna realized she had almost stopped breathing. "There isn't a murder? So, where is Judge Gattino's daughter?"

"Patricia is a senior in high school, and she is in class right where she is supposed to be. We never told her why we were inquiring. She probably thinks her old man is checking up on her." Bowler was still trying to suppress a laugh.

Lou and Donna stared at each other. The horror they had already dealt with over their 'new case' was instantly lifted from their shoulders. Both started laughing.

Officer Bowler stared at them, confused.

"Show us your 'crime' scene, Officer." Lou could hardly contain himself.

Behind the house were a half-dozen officers talking and packing things up to leave. Bowler walked them over to a patio table where the menacing head lay.

There it was. A mannequin head. Neither one of them felt like touching it.

Bowler handed them a senior picture of Patricia Gattino. They gasped at the same time.

The blonde hair color was identical to the photo. It was parted in exactly the right place and held back with a purple barrette duplicating her picture. Both had blue eyes. There was no doubt it was made to look like the judge's daughter.

"I can certainly see why the neighbor thought it was Patricia!" Donna was stunned.

"Does this mannequin belong to the Gattino's?" It was the only question Lou could think of.

"Don't know. Finding out the details would be your job, now wouldn't it?" Officer Bowler chuckled again while he bagged the head and gave it to Donna. "Have fun."

There was a woman standing by some of the officers preparing to leave. Lou walked up to her.

"Excuse me. I am Detective Lou McGregor. Are you the woman who made the call to the police?"

"Yes, yes. I'm Mrs. Woodman, Cindy Woodman, from next door. I am so sorry for bothering you guys. I really thought something was wrong…"

"No problem, Ma'am! I would have done the same thing. I can see why you thought it was the young lady who lives here." Lou was trying his best not to upset her any more than she appeared to be.

Donna joined them and asked, "Did you see anything unusual this morning before the head appeared?"

"No, nothing. This neighborhood is usually pretty quiet. Everyone kind of knows who everyone is, if you know what I mean."

Cindy Woodman continued, "I wouldn't have called the police if the Mrs. had been home. She goes to see her mother this time of the year, you know. Their housekeeper doesn't come on Thursdays – only Monday and Friday, so there wasn't anyone home to call about it."

Just as Donna was about to thank her and walk away, Mrs. Woodman said, "Again, I am sure it is nothing, but I saw the pool cleaner come back here this morning. On Thursdays, I clean my upstairs rooms. That is why I see what is going on from the second floor. Obviously, when you have a pool, you have to keep it clean! We don't have a pool like they do. Otherwise, I really don't know my neighbors personally."

Both Lou and Donna smiled, thanked her, and watched her leave.

"Doesn't know her neighbors personally? She knows everything about them!" Lou just shook his head, wondering if his neighbors knew as much about him.

"Guess there are gossips even in rich areas." Donna knew what Lou was thinking, and it made her chuckle.

"Okay, let's not screw this up just because it looks like a prank, Donna," Lou said. "Let's look around and make a note of anything out of the ordinary."

Donna was surprised at his statement but saw the wisdom in it. "Okay. You have a valid point. Let's do it." She took time to look around the yard.

All of the police officers were now gone. Lou and Donna started checking the scene, making comments in their notebooks. They also took a lot of pictures.

It would be almost impossible to determine if any of the officers damaged anything. However, Donna understood Lou's desire to see if there was anything at all to collect.

There wasn't.

# Chapter 2

"A what? A *doll* head!" Chief Parry shouted into his phone.

"We are on our way to see Judge Gattino at the courthouse before someone else tells him what happened."

"Good idea, Decker." Parry hung up.

"Okay, we're here. I just need to find a parking spot." Lou swung his car into the first one available.

Once inside, they showed their credentials, took the elevator to the court floor and was admitted to the Judge's chambers.

Judge Gattino was surprised to see them.

"Lou, what a surprise to see you. And you brought your beautiful partner with you. Donna, isn't it? What can I do for you, Detectives? I have to be back in court in ten minutes, so make it fast!"

"Sir," Donna knew Lou would leave it to her to explain. "Sir, we just left your house. There had been a call that you had a head floating in your pool," Donna quickly added, "But I assure you it was not human! We just came from there, and it was a mannequin head."

"It looked a lot like your daughter, Patricia," Lou added.

Donna went on to say, "Her school was checked, and she was in class. She is just fine."

"A mannequin? Really? Well, it sounds like a prank to me. Sorry you guys were bothered with it." The judge was not upset.

"We just wanted to let you know before some reporter called and wanted to know how you feel about losing your daughter!" Donna made everyone chuckle this time.

"Okay, but why would anyone think it was my daughter?"

"Oh, sorry. The mannequin head looked just like her! It had the same blonde hair color, hairstyle, and blue eyes. I can understand someone thinking it was her. Do you have any other children who could be playing a prank on her?" Donna started seeing the worry in the Judge's eyes.

" No. No other children. Pet, we call her Pet, is our only child. Where could that head have come from? We don't have any such thing in our house. It sounds creepy to me. Well, I have to go, Detectives. I do appreciate your coming by. And you are right, I probably would have flipped out if some reporter had called me first."

"We will continue to look into it, if it is alright with you, Your Honor." Donna was getting uneasy about it all.

"Of course, of course. Good day, and thanks again."

"Sounds like you arranged to have your pool cleaned this morning. That's always a good thing." Donna was making small talk as they left the judge's chambers.

"No. Not this morning. Our pool cleaner only comes on Saturdays. See you later." Judge Gattino headed away from them.

Lou and Donna stopped short outside the chambers and watched the Judge rush to his courtroom.

"No pool cleaner? Something's wrong here." Lou was feeling the same angst that Donna had mentioned earlier.

As they were leaving the floor, Lou saw a small, odd-looking man with beady eyes, watching them. When the man saw Lou turned his way, he disappeared into the stairway.

On the way down in the elevator, Donna admitted to Lou, "I have an uneasy feeling about this case. Something isn't right."

~~~~~

"So you're telling me you spent the entire day working on the observations of a neighbor woman? Let's see... she saw a teenager's head in the pool. No, wait! It was just a mannequin.

"After deploying a bunch of police officers and detectives, she failed to observe there wasn't any blood in the pool. Then she says she saw a pool cleaner. No, wait! He doesn't come until Saturday.

"Does that just about sum up your day, detectives?" Parry was irritated.

"Yes, sir," Lou said. "But there did seem to be something odd…"

"*ODD?* Something odd about a mannequin head in a pool? I am so glad I have such intelligent people working for me! Now get outta here. First thing in the morning, I want the report that closes this case! Got it? And stop this nonsense of making mountains out of…*nothing!*" Parry waved his arms, and they left his office.

"Uh, that went well…" Donna frowned as she walked back to her desk. She wondered if her gut feelings were wrong about the case. *After all, Pat is eighteen and can do what she wants, can't she?*

After getting their desks cleaned off for the day, Lou smiled and said, "Let's go have dinner!"

Driving their own cars, they headed for her parent's house for dinner. She seldom got off early enough to join them, but tonight was the exception. Her mother had asked Lou to join them, and he was thrilled at another Italian dinner with the Deckers.

Brad and Betty Decker were both of Italian descent, and no one can cook lasagna like her mother. Tonight's the night to indulge.

Donna looked like her beautiful mother, both having ivory skin and near black hair. At five-foot-four and a size six, they both could have been sisters. However, it was the large sapphire blue eyes they shared that could stop traffic.

Conversation at the dinner table was always filled with laughter. They loved having Lou around and pushed him for details of their cases that Donna wouldn't give them.

When she looked at her mother across the table, Donna knew she was seeing herself in twenty years. *Not bad at all,* she thought. Even so, nothing could look as good as the lasagna.

~~~~~

Donna was the first one in on Friday morning, which was usually the case. She was writing out the notes Parry wanted when she saw Lou get out of the elevator.

Just as she was about to speak to him, Parry waved them both into his office. She figured they were about to be assigned another case.

After sitting, Parry was quiet for a couple of minutes. The detectives knew better than to push him.

"She didn't come home last night." Parry's voice was little more than a whisper.

"She didn't... *who* didn't?" Donna didn't like the concerned look on her boss's face.

"Pat. Patricia Gattino. The Judge called me early this morning saying she didn't come home after school. Though it wasn't like her, he let it go until morning thinking she might have been mad at him for the cops showing up at her school. He did have a tendency to be strict with her, so he waited.

"She still didn't come home, and she didn't show up at school this morning. We now have a missing person. You guys get back on it. Interview the neighbor again and see if you can get any more info on this pool cleaner.

"Guess I was kind of hard on you guys yesterday. It looks like we have a problem after all." Parry was talking more to himself than to the others.

"No problem, Boss. We both understood your point of view. I am so sorry to hear about Patricia. However, shouldn't this be turned over to Missing Persons?" Lou didn't understand why they would be assigned this case. There was no homicide that anyone knew of.

"You started it. You'll finish it. Got it?"

"We'll get right on it." That's all Lou needed to hear. He got up and added, "We will be leaving for Vickridge now."

Parry nodded as they were leaving his office. "And tell Duncan and Palmer to get in here. I have a new case for them, too."

Donna informed her detective friends to see Parry, while Lou got his car around to the front. She joined him as he pulled up.

Twenty minutes later, they arrived in Vickridge. They went first to Cindy Woodman's house, where she invited them in for coffee.

"I didn't really get a good look at him. I mean, I assumed he was the pool cleaner. He wore a uniform and was by the pool, so I just thought he was cleaning.

"I mean, I saw him once. Then after dusting all the furniture in my back bedroom, I glanced out again. He was gone, but that's when I saw that horrible head.

"I don't know of anyone who didn't like that family. Except maybe for this young guy who got asked to leave. Actually, it was more like he was told to go. It happened about a month or two ago.

"He was really angry with Patricia. They were out by the pool and boy, were they going at it. She finally yelled at him to leave, and he stomped out of the backyard by the side gate." Cindy chuckled at the memory.

"Ma'am, do you know this guy or what they were mad about?" Lou was paying attention to every word.

"No, I don't know who he was. He was probably her age, but I didn't get a good look at his face. Even so, I can tell you he was furious with her. I couldn't tell what words they were saying until the girl yelled for him to leave."

"That's okay, Ma'am. Thank you for the information. Now, back to the pool cleaner. Can you remember anything else about him? Just think really hard. Was there anything unusual about him or around him?" Lou was hoping for anything to work with.

"No. Well, he had a tattoo on his left arm, but then, everyone does these days, don't they? This one was a bit unusual in that it looked like a heart. Not an elaborate one, but a simple outline. Not the sort of thing you usually see on a man's arm, if you know what I mean. Something in the center of it, but he was too far away for me to see what it was.

"And he was constantly looking down, which is why I never saw his face, and why I thought he was the pool cleaner. He faced downward all the time," she said.

Unable to get more information, they said their goodbyes.

# Chapter 3

After leaving Woodman's house, they went next door and rang the bell. Judge Gattino answered.

"Come in Lou. Come in. Hi, Donna. Here is where I say I am sorry to see you again. I… I am not sure what to make of any of this. I have taken some time off from work. Other judges will have to fill in.

"Gracie will be here in an hour or so. She left her mother's immediately when I called her this morning. It's only three hours from Kansas City, as you know.

"So, Parry was telling me that my neighbors, the Woodman's, saw a pool cleaner here yesterday. No, no. Only Saturdays. I have to tell you I am more than a little worried." The Judge seemed withdrawn, and his voice was quiet. He was almost talking to himself.

After they were all sitting in the family room, facing the swimming pool outside, Lou took over.

"Have you contacted the pool company? Could they have sent someone out because Saturday wasn't available? Anything like that?"

"No. I mean yes. I talked with them and, no, they did not send anyone out yesterday. Saturday is still scheduled. It wasn't them."

Donna spoke up. "It seems whoever was here, was the one who put the mannequin head in the pool. He apparently wanted to appear to be a pool cleaner because he was in some kind of uniform. The neighbor never saw his face.

"Needless to say, I have to ask if there is anyone who would want to get back at you for something."

"Donna, I am a Criminal Court Judge. Practically everyone who enters my court can leave with a grudge! Just add everyone in Wichita to your list, plus anyone I have put in jail."

"I understand, but has there been a recent incident that could have caused someone to want to get even with you?" Lou injected.

"No. Oh, I don't know. Not that I can think of."

Donna thought about the argument the neighbor saw. "Is Patricia dating anyone? Does she bring guys over here, maybe to swim?"

"No. I mean she has in the past, but she really is looking forward to college, so she stopped dating altogether a couple of months back. I didn't care one way or another. But, I have to tell you, as her father, I was glad to hear she wants to concentrate on her education."

Donna was walking around the family room, looking at all the pictures of Patricia hanging on the walls, with and without her parents.

"How about your wife? Any problems there?" Lou was making notes of everything said.

"What are you implying? My wife has no enemies!"

"Sorry, sir, but I have to ask." Lou was shocked by his reaction but knew he was under a great deal of pressure.

"Yeah, yeah. I know. Sorry about raising my voice. I just can't think of anything that would cause someone to hate me enough to kidnap my daughter unless it is for ransom. But there have been no demands."

Donna added, "Let's hope she is just staying with a friend and will show up soon. It's just procedure, but we will need a list of all the employees you work with at the courthouse."

"I figured you would. I already have a list." The judge handed it to Donna.

"Please call us if she comes home." Lou handed him his card, and they left.

As they were leaving Vickridge, Donna called in the request to have patrol officers question each of the judge's neighbors about what they possibly saw or heard.

Their next stop was Patricia's high school. With help from the secretary in the office, they found the senior class she was supposed to be in at this time of day.

"Pay attention, class. This will be on your test. If you use the adverb as ...,"

The English teacher stopped talking and glanced at the two detectives when they walked into her classroom.

"We apologize for imposing, but we would like to speak to your class for a moment, if we may." Donna was generally the one to speak in front of groups.

The teacher smiled and motioned them up front.

"As you may have heard, Patricia Gattino did not make it home last night. We are here to find out if any of you would know her whereabouts." Donna glanced around the room, watching the teenagers eyes.

No one spoke up, so she continued, "We don't care if she ran away, is hiding somewhere, or is staying with friends. We don't care. She is eighteen years old and can do what she wants. She is not in any kind of trouble with the law. We are only concerned about her safety, so if you know anything, please tell us."

Slowly, one hand rose in the back of the room.

Donna pointed at her and said, "Yes. Please stand."

A tall, lanky girl stood. "I don't know where she is now, but I saw her get into a car after school yesterday."

"What's your name?"

"Karen."

"Karen, do you know whose car it was?"

"No, ma'am."

"Can you describe the car?"

"Blue. Not new, but looked okay. I mean it wasn't junky or anything. A Ford, I think. You know, one of those little ones that get a lot of mileage?"

"Can you tell me what the driver looked like?"

"No, I couldn't see through the tinted windows. I don't remember if I have ever seen that car before, but there are so many parked out front after school. I just saw her talking to him through the passenger's window and then she got in."

"Thank you, Karen. Did anyone else see anything yesterday?"

Donna got no response, so she changed course.

"Does anyone know if she has a boyfriend?"

A young man in front spoke up.

"Uh, no. At least not that I know of."

"And your name?"

"Brian. Brian Parker. I *was* her boyfriend until about three months ago when we both realized we had different dreams for the future. So we stopped being a couple. We remained really close friends, though. I would know if she had another guy.

"Pat is a wonderful girl, and I am worried about her now." Brian was staring at his desktop.

"And you didn't see her after school yesterday?"

Brian looked at the teacher and then said, "Uh, no. I had to stay after school because I didn't have my English homework done."

The class chuckled. Donna glanced at the teacher, who nodded her head as she smiled.

Lou started down the rows, passing out business cards.

"Okay, thank you all for your time. If you think of anything you saw or heard, anything at all, call the number on the back of the cards my good-looking partner is handing out. His name is Lou, by the way." Donna was smiling at Lou.

*He really is good looking. I couldn't work with a better guy.* Donna forced her thoughts back to the situation at hand.

Several girls said, "Hello, Lou," which caused chuckles.

"We are grateful for your help. Don't forget to call if you remember something – no matter how minor it may seem. We need to make sure Pat is safe."

With that, they said their goodbyes to the class.

Before leaving, Donna said, "Brian, would you step outside into the hall for a moment?"

Once in the hall and the classroom door was shut, Brian became belligerent.

"*What?* Why are you picking on *me?*"

Lou wasn't sure why Donna wanted to speak with him, so he deferred to her.

"A neighbor saw you in a bad argument with Pat about a month or so ago, in her backyard. What was that all about, Brian?" Donna stared at him.

"What? So we argued, so what? My dad's an attorney, and I don't have to talk to you!" Brian shoved the classroom door open and walked in leaving Lou and Donna staring at each other.

"That was different. How did you know he was the one arguing with Pat?" Lou led Donna down the hall and out the door.

"I didn't. I just took a chance hoping he would fess up to it. We now know he was the one there, but we still don't know what the yelling was about."

On the way back to the station, Lou was quiet.

"Okay, what's up? I know that look." Donna could read her friend like a book.

"Nothing really… just that Brian kid. Did he get pissed off when she broke up with him? I'm just thinking out loud here. Could that be what the argument was all about? Him trying to get her back?"

"Could be. I'd say 'most likely.' He said they both agreed to the breakup, but that doesn't mean that's the way it happened. We will check him out, too. However, he has an alibi for after school, but that doesn't mean he didn't have a friend pick her up and he joined them later."

# Chapter
# 4

Lou looked tired. "We missed lunch. Wanna get something to eat before we head to the courthouse?"

"Burger sounds good."

"So," Lou grinned at his partner. "You really think I am 'good looking?'" He fluttered his eyes at her.

"Drive, old man, drive." Donna loved teasing him about being forty years old. At thirty-two, she always used the 'age' card when she could. *Even so, I can't deny he is one sexy guy!*

Lou pulled up to a McDonalds, and they went in to order. Sitting at a table near the back, they dug into their food.

After eating for a while, Lou watched his partner's face for clues. "What do you think so far?"

"What can I think? I am pretty sure she didn't instigate this disappearance. Just a gut feeling. Being eighteen she doesn't have a reason to hide somewhere. She could just have told her dad she was angry and leaving for a while. No, this doesn't look good."

"I hear ya. We need... *CRAP!* A TV truck just pulled up out front. Let's get out of here!" Lou had little tolerance for the media messing in his cases.

They grabbed their drinks and headed through the door.

"Detectives! Have you found Gattino's body? Who do you think did it?"

Lou swung on the man talking. "Do you *know* she is dead, mister? *DO* you? No? Then shut up. What we know at this time is an adult is missing. That is it. And if I find you following us again, I will have you arrested for interfering in a police investigation. That's jail time, bozo. *Got it?*"

They jumped into his car and left. He watched his rear-view mirror all the way to the courthouse. No van.

Donna laughed out loud. "Boy, I guess you told him a thing or two! Bozo, was it? I loved it!"

"Don't get me started on the media…," Lou was gritting his teeth.

Once again, being shown the judge's chambers, they sat down with his secretary, Mary Watson.

Lou started with, "Mary, look at this list of employees the judge states he works with or around. Is it complete, to your knowledge?"

After carefully reading it, she nodded.

"Do you know of anyone who hated the judge? Had a grievance? Or felt betrayed? Anything?"

"No, I really don't, Detective. You know him. He is the kindest man. Not a mean bone in his body. Maybe someone he sent to jail, but I can't think of anyone who worked with him that didn't like him. Of course, there is Jason, who really dislikes Patricia, but that has nothing to do with the judge…"

"Whaa… Jason who?" It was Donna who jumped on this information.

"Oh, Jason Sullivan. He works for Judge Carollton down the hall."

"Is he in today? Can we talk to him?"

"Sure. I will go get him right now." Mary stood and left the room.

Lou's eyes were big. "You don't think it wasn't the judge they were after, but Patricia herself, do you?"

"I don't know. Anything is possible at this point. I can't wait to hear what that problem was!" Donna was just as surprised by this unexpected news.

Within ten minutes, Mary returned with Jason. She introduced everyone then left Judge Gattino's office.

"Mary said you detectives want to talk to me. What do you want?" Jason was nervous. He was in his mid-twenties, about five-seven in height, and definitely not a very good-looking guy. Small eyes and ears made the rest of his round face seem huge.

Lou recognized him right away. He was the man who ducked into the stairway when he saw Lou looking at him yesterday.

*He's hiding from something… or someone.*

"Sit, Jason. My name is Detective Lou McGregor, and this is my partner, Detective Donna Decker."

He nodded to them both and sat down.

"As you have probably heard, Patricia Gattino is missing. Do you know anything about that?" Lou took charge of this interview.

"Oh, yeah, I heard about that, but why should I know anything?" For some reason, he seemed happy to talk about this subject.

"We understand you didn't like her too much."

"Patricia? I couldn't stand her. She was a spoiled, self-centered brat, who thought she was better than me." Jason's face showed his anger.

"Why is that exactly, Jason?"

"I asked her out once. You should have seen her face! Pat acted like I was the worst thing on earth and the last person she would ever go out with. She didn't say in so many words, but I got the message when she turned me down flat!

"After that, whenever she came here, she avoided me like the plague! The stuck-up bi…" Jason looked over at Donna and didn't finish.

"When was the last time you saw her?"

"It's been about two weeks. I don't see her every time she's here. I don't want to see her. Besides, I only work here part-time - three half days a week, so I don't know how often she was here."

Lou stood up and offered his hand. "Thank you for taking the time to speak with us, Mr. Sullivan. We appreciate it."

Jason shook Lou's hand, then smiled at Donna and left.

Lou sat back down and looked at his partner. Both brains were moving too fast to talk.

After several moments of thinking it through, Lou told Donna about seeing him the day before. No doubt about it, this man is a suspect.

"This guy strikes me as the type that would plan ahead to get even. What do you think? He was obviously nervous when he first came in."

"Yeah, I saw that too. But, a lot of people are nervous when police want to talk to them, so you can't really hold that against him. But, did you hear what he said about Patricia? I mean *really* hear? He spoke about her in the past tense – 'who thought she was better than me.' Why wouldn't she *still* think the same, unless he *knows* she's dead? That bugs me."

"Wow. You're right. I didn't catch that. He could be our guy!"

After making sure their notes about Jason were finished, Lou called Mary back in.

"Okay, whoever is next on that list, see if they can come in."

Mary nodded and left her boss's office.

There were five more interviews. No one had a bad word for Judge Gattino or his family. They thanked Mary and left.

At the precinct, they filled the boss in on their interview with the judge, their stop at the school, then the courthouse.

After getting the full day's report done, they requested background checks on all the employees of the school as well as Brian Parker and Jason Sullivan. Right now, Brian and Jason held top spots for Pat being missing.

Checking criminal records was easy. They found both Brian and Jason had arrests for drugs. Brian's was a few months ago. Apparently, his father got it all hushed up since he is still a minor at seventeen.

As for Jason, it was two years back. It was his first, so he was given probation. Nothing else was there. Not even a parking ticket. In fact, Jason didn't even own a car.

By the time they had gone over the new information, it was late. They said their goodbyes to each other and headed home.

Donna knew there wasn't a chance of getting any good Italian food tonight.

~~~

Saturday morning found them both going over their notes. Lou spoke to the judge and confirmed his daughter was still missing, and they had not heard from her. The detectives also received the report from the officers who canvassed the judge's neighborhood the day before. Nothing of help came from their efforts.

Lou noticed his partner seemed down, but didn't want to interfere until she felt like talking. A couple of times she looked as if she would break down and cry. He had never seen her so upset.

*Could a missing petite, blonde girl have hit her this hard? Possible. We don't usually work a missing person case.* Lou was becoming increasingly concerned about his friend and partner.

After about an hour, he said, "You wanna talk about it?"

She choked back a tear and shook her head and said, "No."

Shortly after ten, Donna's phone rang.

"Detective, this is Officer Blain. I am told you are assigned the Patricia Gattino case. I wanted to inform you we found her purse this morning. Before you ask, it is hers alright. Her driver's license and cell phone are inside. She had about thirty bucks, too, so it doesn't seem like robbery."

"Where did you find it, officer?"

"It was laying on the banks of the Arkansas River in downtown. You know, just north of Kellogg, but before Lewis St."

"Thank you very much. Bag it carefully and get the purse to the lab as soon as you can. Maybe we can get prints or DNA." Donna knew this one item was proof she didn't leave on her own.

*A girl doesn't go anywhere without her purse, let alone her cell phone. She didn't go off on her own. This has to be kidnapping. But why? No ransom had been demanded...*

She informed Lou and asked him to tell Parry, while she went back to the school background checks that had come in. Not everyone was there, but she was anxious to see what they had.

Lou came back and sat at his desk, facing hers. "Parry is as sickened as we are." His voice was almost a whisper. With that evidence, their case had taken an unfortunate turn.

A high school gym teacher had a domestic violence charge against him three years prior. He was definitely put on the suspect list. Violence can erupt anywhere. Otherwise, the school information delivered nothing.

# Chapter 5

Sometime in the afternoon Lou's best friend, Detective Roger Duncan, stopped by their desks. "Hey, you guys, don't forget tonight is our B-B-Q."

"You bet. How many are coming this time?" Lou brightened up. All day on the paperwork was not his thing.

"As usual, everyone in our department is invited for 'homicide detectives' night. Two are in

Kansas City, and two are working tonight. I know Gary is on vacation. However, whoever shows up will be fine with me. " Roger smiled at his friend. He cared deeply for Lou. The difference in skin color didn't matter to either one.

At six-foot, he didn't quite reach Lou's height, but Roger unfailingly accused him of adding lifts to his shoes, just so he could look taller than him. It always got a laugh from anyone who heard it.

Roger married Angelina, the love of his life, last year and Lou was his best man. Donna was also the Maid of Honor. These two were loved in the Duncan family.

They had this type of cookout about every six weeks or so, whenever he felt the gang needed it. Getting everyone together gave him and his co-workers a chance to relax and unwind. They talked about their cases, ask for advice, looked at some clues from a different perspective. It really helped him and his friends.

The spouses had their own pleasant time for movie night, inside. Angelina always found ways to make their time together special. That left the detectives a chance to be forthcoming with information they couldn't mention in front of others.

Lou was ready for another great time at his friend's house in Eastborough. Roger used to live close to Lou in Woodlawn Village but moved when he married Angelina, and adopted her little girl, Taylor, who was now four.

Angelina inherited a lot of money and an expensive home in Eastborough, another east-side wealthy neighborhood. Roger got teased a lot about living the high life, but he took it well.

After work, Donna dropped her car at her townhouse and went with Lou to Duncan's house. Their home was beautiful and had the most elegant doorbell chimes Donna had ever heard. She always wanted to be the one to ring the bell.

Angelina opened the door and gave them a big hug, directing them out into the backyard where their co-workers were lounging around.

It was nice to be in the company of people who understood your daily stress. Some came alone, and some brought wives, who stayed together in the house. They liked being able to give their spouses a chance to unwind after hours.

Roger's partner, J.C. Palmer brought his wife, Julie. J.C. stood for James Casey, but he had been called by his initials since he was a pup. At forty-eight, he had been on the force for twenty-five years but was still in good shape.

Julie immediately hooked up with Angelina and another wife as they cut up snacks in the kitchen and planned what movie they wanted to watch in the theater room.

Along for the ride was J.C.'s daughter, Karlene Palmer. At twenty-two, she had been a police officer for almost a year. Her parents called her Karlie, but the officers she worked with called her K.T.

She wanted to be a detective like her father someday and came along to learn. No one minded her presence as she was under the same rule not to repeat what she heard.

Lou and Donna found extra chairs next to J.C. and his daughter, while Roger rounded up some sweet tea to drink for the new arrivals. He knew they both didn't drink alcohol. Truth is, Roger didn't drink much, anymore.

Next, he called them over to the grill to pick out their choice of steaks, chicken burgers, dogs, or veggie burgers. The nearby table held mashed potatoes, veggies, salads, chips, rolls and dessert.

While looking over the food and making choices, Donna leaned over to Lou and whispered, "It is just me, or does Karlie look like she's fifteen years old?"

Lou chuckled out loud. "That, my dear, is what happens when you get old. *Everyone* starts looking underage!"

Donna sighed, made the last of her food selections, then went back to the group.

From time to time, Angelina would run out to the grill for more food. She was greeted with whistles and cheers. She would smile and curtsy before going back inside. Roger's love for her was written all over his face for anyone to see.

Once seated, Lou enjoyed half his food, then asked about Roger's new case.

J.C. was the first to respond between bites, "Oh, Lou, senseless is the only way to describe it."

"Seems a woman in her fifties was murdered in her car." Roger was shaking his head. "It doesn't make any sense. Reva, her name was Reva Jane Walters, worked for a dental clinic on

Webb Road. Had for almost thirty years. She was very well-liked by her co-workers.

"So far, we can't find anything that would put her in danger. We don't know if she was targeted or just in the wrong place..."

J.C. came back, "Or if she was attacked by a jilted lover. From the pictures we have seen, she was a pretty woman. Hank Lawrence was her boyfriend, and he's definitely on our radar. What about your case, Dale? How are you guys doing?"

Dale glanced over at his partner, Steve, and said, "Oh don't look at us! We just locked up our last case. So far, Parry hasn't yelled for us!" Dale's comments brought laughter from the group. They all knew how that worked.

Lou asked, "Remind me of that last case...?"

"Remember, the mother that refused to loan her son any more money? He killed her for the inheritance, but didn't realize she had changed her will and left him nothing! Just as well, he wouldn't have been able to spend it in prison anyway! " Dale was smiling.

Lou nodded, "Wasn't he into drugs or something that he needed a constant flow of cash?"

"Close. It was gambling. He lost a great deal and owed a great deal. The problem was, the money he kept losing was his mother's, and she just got tired of it. She wasn't rich by any means but was comfortable, that is if her son didn't throw it all away."

Steve jumped in with, "When he saw the evidence we had against him, he confessed, pleaded guilty and got life without parole just two days ago. It serves him right. Who kills their own mother, and for money on top of that?"

"What did she do with her money?" Lou had finished his delicious meal and was considering seconds.

"It went to the Kansas Humane Society, right here in Wichita. Every last dime. I, for one, think she made an excellent choice. I love animals, especially dogs." Dale was smiling to himself.

"When I want another dog, I always go there to give a poor unwanted guy a loving home. I don't need a purebred for hundreds or thousands of dollars. I want a *real* dog!"

Everyone laughed, but Dale added that sometimes you found purebreds there too. Adoption costs were higher, but even people who had paid big bucks for a highly bred animal can turn their backs on them.

"Because some irresponsible dog owner decided they couldn't be bothered with them any longer. These are living creatures they are throwing away!"

Getting Dale away from his favorite rant, Lou turned to J.C., "I have never asked you before, but I really want to know. How in the world did you get that terrible scar above your eyebrow?"

Karlie laughed out loud. J.C. chuckled at her, then turned to Lou.

"What 'terrible scar?' I have you know that is my Badge of Honor! Okay, it happened about seven years ago, I think. I was on a beat back then, and I was driving by an alley when I saw this man beating on this young lady. I jammed on the brakes, jumped out and ran to them. He was screaming at her that she was ' a dead woman,' when I knocked him down from behind.

"So, then he jumped up and turned his knife on me. I got this slash on my face about the time my gun went off, ending the problem.

"The girl, Mary Louise Quinton, was nineteen years old and had been held captive by this drugged up pimp. He forced Mary to take drugs and made her a sex slave to get money for his drugs. She tried to run away that night, but he caught her and was going to kill her for it. That caused the confrontation that I got into.

"Anyway, I call this scar my Badge of Honor because I helped her get clean, back on her feet, and return to school. She is now a school teacher helping other kids stay off the street. The end result doesn't get any better than that, my friends!" J.C. rubbed his scar while smiling.

Karlie smiled, leaned in and nudged her father affectionately.

Dale gave him a high five and turned to Lou. "What about you guys? I heard you got a new case."

Donna's head was down, deep in thought, so Lou spoke up. "Judge Frank Gattino's eighteen-year-old daughter is missing."

Roger let out a low whistle. "Whoa. No pressure there…"

Donna finally joined the conversation, "They found a mannequin head that looked like Patricia, the daughter, floating in their swimming pool earlier in the day, before she went missing.

Looks like someone was trying to tell us something, but I don't like thinking about what that story may be. Her purse was found this morning near the river downtown. It contained her cell phone, too, so it appears she didn't leave on her own."

"No kidding. Have any suspects?"

"Some. We are looking at an ex-boyfriend, a guy who was spurned by her, and maybe a sicko teacher. Plus, a judge could have thousands of enemies."

They all agreed with her assessment of judges.

"The problem we have here," Donna continued, "is we don't know if she is alive or deceased. We are spending all of our time assuming she is dead. So we are looking at people who may have had a reason to kill her. But what if she is not dead? What if she was just kidnapped?

"That means the reason for her disappearance would be totally different, and that means our suspects are not suspects!"

# Chapter
# 6

Making a trip back to the grill, Lou grabbed a hot dog and some chips for seconds.

After returning to his seat, he asked Roger, "How did this Reva woman die? No mannequins, I hope."

J.C. jumped in, "Oh please! How did she *not* die? We don't have the official report yet, but it could have been the stab wounds, or the bullet in her head, or the strangulation marks on her throat. Your guess is as good as ours. She had numerous bruises showing she put up one heck of a fight. That's for sure. The perp had to have gotten some bruises of his own. The only thing we don't think happened was rape. She was fully dressed, and it did not appear to be a sexual attack. But that's just our observation."

In a quiet voice, Donna said, "At least *that* is good news. She was intelligent and hard-working. A lot of people counted on her, especially Dr. Rong."

Silence reigned. Everyone stared at Donna, as she continued.

"And yes, she was as beautiful as her name. She didn't look her age at all. There isn't anything she wouldn't do for you if she could. How can a person like that be murdered with such rage?" Donna was at the breaking point once again.

The silence continued, giving her time to compose herself again.

Lou was the first to speak, "You *knew* her…?"

"Yes. We were good friends, actually. I thought of her as the sister I never had. Marvin, uh, Dr. Marvin Rong called me last night after I got home from work. He was distraught but called to see if I knew, yet.

"I have been going to Marvin for dental care for over ten years. There was just a strong friendship from the start with Reva. We would have lunch together, whenever we could. We called or would text the fun things going on in our lives. We didn't have to be in the same room to enjoy each other's company. Our time apart seemed to bring us closer together, if that makes any sense.

"With her work schedule, plus a daughter and grandchild living in her house, her time was limited, like mine. However, we always found a way to touch base every month or two.

"I doubt you will find her boyfriend had anything to do with it. He loved her, and I'm sure he is devastated. Everyone who knew her is devastated… Be certain to let me know what the autopsy says was the cause of death."

The silence continued for a couple more minutes. No one knew what to say. Karlie had her hand over her mouth while staring at the ground. She looked like she was holding back tears.

Lou reached over and took Donna's hand, and she squeezed his. Her pain was evident.

Wanting to lighten the mood, Roger piped up with, "So we have an intelligent, hard-working woman, with no enemies, dead in her car. You have a missing girl who may or may not be deceased or have a missing head. Boy, I think I need another drink."

Roger stood, and everyone held up their own glass for refills.

~~~~~

Lou and Donna both had off Sunday. Lou's mother, Darlene, wanted them over to lounge around the pool. Donna thought it was a great way to spend a late April day. She needed relief from the stress and grief she felt, even if only for a few hours.

Darlene lived just two blocks from her son, Lou, in Woodlawn Village. With all her money, she could live anywhere she liked, but the fact she didn't try to impress anyone made Donna love her more. She was a wonderful woman.

She is also the reason Lou was so wealthy. Darlene came into a lot of money when Lou was just a boy. Being a beautiful, light-skinned, black woman, she attracted the attention of a white boy. They ran off and got married. Thus Lou was conceived. The marriage didn't work out, but Darlene made the most of it. Lou's father died in a car crash just a few years after the divorce.

Darlene, being incredibly smart, invested the money she had obtained from a lawsuit, to take care of herself and her son for the rest of their lives.

Lou didn't have to work if he didn't want to, but he loved his job. With a closet full of $2,000 suits and a Mercedes in the drive, he looked like a cop on the take, if you didn't know him better. He dressed like a corporate CEO instead of a detective.

His mother had a swimming pool at her home, and Lou didn't, so it was easy to get her son to come to visit when the weather was nice and warm.

It was mid-afternoon when Donna got out of the pool and laid back on the lounger. Her eyes were closed, and Lou dominated her thoughts as he did so often these days. She knew she was falling in love with her partner, but she continually tried to deny it. It was now at a point she couldn't ignore it any longer.

She had known for some time Lou was in love with her. Oh, he didn't say so, but she knew it.

That, too, she tried to deny for the longest time. Just the way he looked at her told how he felt.

Loving him was easy. What's not to love? He was the epitome of tall, dark and handsome. His light skin set off his black hair and dark-brown eyes. At his height, he made her feel safe when he was close to her. What woman doesn't want that?

She also knew being in love with your partner was the last thing any detective would want. It could cause a conflict of interest on the job. Donna would not be allowed to work with him anymore if she made her feelings known.

The department thought such arrangements would cause the detectives to make errors on the job in order to protect the partner. Maybe so, but one thing is for sure. They could never work together again, and Donna didn't think she could stand that.

Good reason to keep quiet.

~~~~~

Monday found them rested and ready to work. She couldn't remember when she had seen Lou look so relaxed and happy. It made her heart skip a beat.

The rest of the background checks came in, and they were devouring them as fast as they could.

Researching cases during the last year, they had come up with four men who didn't like the outcome of being in court with the judge. Three had an appointment to be interviewed.

The first to be interviewed was Barry Gattrem, an aircraft mechanic at forty-two. He had been charged with stealing a neighbor's B-B-Q grill. It had been found in his backyard after police were called by the victim. Barry and his neighbor had problems going way back.

"I didn't do it! That son-of-a... he lied! He put that grill in my backyard just to frame me!"

"Okay," Lou started, "What happened in court?"

"That judge found me guilty because I had 'possession of stolen property' and fined me $1,000! One thousand! I didn't do anything wrong!"

"So, did it make you mad enough to want to hurt the judge?"

"Hurt... hey, I don't know what is going on here, but if that judge is dead, it ain't me! I was mad, but I'm no killer!"

"Naw," Lou continued, "The judge isn't dead, Barry. We just need to find out if you are pissed off enough to want your $1,000 back?"

"Yeah, I would like my money back. Who wouldn't? So what?"

Donna chimed in, "The 'so what' is the judge's daughter is missing, and we thought maybe you wanted some ransom money..."

"You can't blame this on me, too. I didn't even know he had a daughter. I sure wouldn't risk going to prison for $1,000! Did that swine of a neighbor say I did? "

"No, Mr. Gattrem, your neighbor has nothing to do with this. Just tell us where you were on Thursday afternoon?"

"Thurs…, I don't… OH! Thursday! My wife and I were in counseling. A once a week thing she insists on. I don't know why. I work at Spirit Aircraft and get off at three. The appointment is from four 'til five on that day. It's a total waste of time and money."

"Write down the counselor's name and phone number, please. We will check it out."

Donna had to ask one last question, "If you and your neighbor hate each other so much, why don't you just move?"

"Lord, woman, you sound just like my wife. I'm not going to let that slime-ball win! He would love for me to move! *He's* the one that needs to move!" With that, Barry got up and stomped out.

# Chapter
# 7

Next was nineteen-year-old Marven Watkins. Judge sent him to jail for six months for car theft and had served his time.

"Mad at the judge? Judge Gattino? You have got to be kidding? I love that man! Sending me to jail was the best thing he could have done – AND giving me a minimum sentence was the second thing!

"Hey, I was out of control. I just didn't have any guidance. Prison changed me. I didn't want to spend my life there, and I knew I had to change. Do you know the Judge came to see me twice in that six months? Really. He was so supportive and wanted me to get my life turned around. I did, too!

"I didn't know he had a daughter, but I'll bet she is really proud of her father."

"Where were you last Thursday afternoon?"

"I was in my AA meeting. I go there to make sure I will never do drugs or alcohol again. I don't want to disappoint myself or the judge.

After writing down the AA location, they said goodbye to Marven.

The third man, Fifty-two-year-old Jason Franken, moved to Arizona a few months back. After a 30-day stint in jail for drunk driving, he requested to go where he had family who could help him. The judge granted his request. They checked with Arizona authorities to make sure he was there.

"Okay, scratch him off the list." Lou only had one name left.

"When does Harley Borden come in?"

"Hold your horses, big boy. He'll be here in thirty minutes." Donna smiled at her partner.

"What do we know about him?

"He was accused of raping his girlfriend at the time. He chose to not have a jury trial because he felt they would bury him.

"The judge felt the man was guilty, but knew there wasn't enough evidence to throw the book at him. So, he found him guilty of the lesser offense of sexual assault and put him in jail for six months. After that, he has two years of community service to do. And of course, a restraining order to never go close to his ex-girlfriend again. And to top it off... he got out last month.

"How's that for mister nice guy?" Donna already didn't like this man.

Dale appeared at their desks.

"Hey, guys. Had a great time Saturday. Thanks for being a part of it. Did you hear what happened over in Butler County last week?"

Donna looked up. "I heard something on the late news, but I don't remember much about it. Wasn't it in El Dorado?"

Lou jumped in, "Yeah. Anyway, El Dorado is where the family lived. However, they found the fourteen-year-old daughter of Sheriff Deputy Sterling Wallace, hanging from a tree out at El Dorado Lake, a few miles away."

Dale added, "I have a friend who works there, and he knows Wallace. He said she committed suicide and left a note. It said something like 'If I can't have my Daddy, I don't want to live.' My friend said Sterling has taken time off from work.

He is devastated that his daughter didn't think he was there enough for her.

"Her name was Alani, and she was their only daughter. The Wallace's have two sons, Jerod at fifteen, and Damion is seventeen. Sterling has been on the force for less than two years. Can you believe it? I can't imagine what those parents are going through."

He walked off shaking his head. Lou and Donna sat staring at each other.

*He's right. Those parents must be falling apart. What is happening to our children, God? Why would they want to die? Are you listening?* Donna knew the same thoughts were running around Lou's brain, too.

Right on time, Harley Borden got off the elevator. They showed him to an interrogation room.

"I don't know why I'm here. I have done my time, and I am doing the community service, as stupid as that is." Harley did not look like a man who ever smiled.

Lou started, "Okay Harley. You are here to tell us what you think of Judge Gattino."

"That idiot? What a waste of taxpayer's dollars. He'll never get my vote!"

"Don't care for him, huh?"

"Why should I. He found me guilty and now I have to register as a sex offender for the rest of my life. How would you like that?"

Donna started with, "Yep. That's what rape will do for you."

"What do you know, sister? You women think you're a man most of the time. I don't have to talk to no female, now do I?" Harley was whining to Lou.

Donna got up and left the room. They had been through this before. When a man hates women, as this guy seemed to, it was easier to get information from him without her there.

"Well now, Harley," Lou knew it was up to him, "have you been to the judge's house lately, say last Thursday?"

"His house? Why would I go to his house? I don't even know where in Vickridge he lives."

Lou caught that immediately. "So you know he lives in Vickridge!"

Harley knew he had said too much. "Yeah, so? Doesn't everyone know where that stuck-up guy lives?"

"Where were you last Thursday afternoon, Harley."

"I don't know. I don't remember. And unless I am under arrest, I am leaving." Harley got up and left the room.

Lou was stewing when Donna returned.

"Guess he doesn't like talking to women or men." She smiled at her frustrated partner.

"Yeah, but I am going to put a tail on him. That man would gladly do something to hurt the judge." Lou's thoughts were not pretty. He was sure he had a live one with this loser.

After making a call to have Borden followed, he received a callback.

"Hey, McGregor. How are you these days? I hear you met our boy, Harley Borden. What's your problem with him?" It was Detective Clayton from Narcotics.

"Hey. I don't hear from you very often. Borden is a suspect in a kidnapping that happened last Thursday afternoon. He was belligerent and didn't want to talk about where he was then."

Detective Clayton chuckled. "I can give you his alibi, Lou. He was working a drug deal down on South Broadway, almost to Haysville. He has been under our surveillance for weeks now.

"We are trying to get his supplier before we arrest him. Sorry to say, but this dude isn't your kidnapper."

Lou took a moment to soak all of that in. "To tell you the truth, I'm glad he's going to go down for something, cause I didn't like one thing about that weasel."

They both chuckled and ended the call. Lou told Donna about losing one of their suspects, but thankfully, Harley wouldn't be on the streets for long.

For the next three days, Lou and Donna interviewed everyone on their list as well as reading more reports on cases from the judge's courtroom.

The ex-boyfriend had an alibi. He was held after school by his English teacher. Nevertheless, the possibility of having a friend involved kept him on the list.

When they questioned Vernon Colter, the teacher with the domestic violence record, he was in shock at being interviewed. They met him after school was out for the day.

"You can't be serious! You suspect me in the case of a missing high school girl because of the fuss my ex-girlfriend made years ago?

"Sir, we have to question everyone, so just settle down!" Lou wasn't in the mood to be jumped on.

"Alright! Fine," he took a deep breath and after a moment spoke quietly. "Look, that domestic 'case' was when I learned my live-in girlfriend had been cheating on me, and I told her to move out. She didn't want to, so I grabbed all of her clothes and personal items and threw them all out on the front lawn.

"Right there in the yard, she started beating on me with her fists, and I held her arms tight, keeping her from hitting me anymore. A neighbor saw what was going on and called the police.

"Of course, she said I hit her, which I didn't, but she had red marks on her arms where I was holding her, so I got arrested. After Police talked with the neighbor who saw her hitting me, they let me go and told my ex to leave the property.

"End of story: I haven't let any woman move into my house since. And I know nothing about this senior girl that's missing. She isn't in any of my classes, and I wouldn't know her if I walked past her."

His story matched what the police report said, so they thanked him for his time and left.

Donna asked, "What do you think? Could he have done this?"

"I doubt it. I really do. The man was cleared of any wrongdoing, and there hasn't been another incident. We can keep him on the list. For now, I am going to put him at the bottom of mine.

"I think I will keep him a little further up on my list." Donna didn't know why, but she wasn't ready to rule him out. Not yet.

"Okay, back to the list of possible enemies the judge may have."

After a couple of hours going through persons who might have a grudge against the judge, Donna looked up and saw Reva's boyfriend, Hank Lawrence, get off the elevator. Roger was there to meet him.

That threw Donna back to the loss of her dear friend. She became angry and swore she would see whoever did this would pay, and pay dearly.

For two days, they worked the files independently. Lou and Donna made up a list of possible suspects on their own, and it was time to compare notes.

Just as they were getting comfortable in Interview Room Two, Dale came in.

"Hey, I thought you might want to know. The Walters woman died from the gunshot in the head. The coroner released the  body this morning, and I heard the family will have the funeral on Friday at Lakeview."

"Thanks, J.C., I appreciate the heads up. I will definitely be at the funeral." At least her friend could now be at peace.

"Oh, we will be there, too. Many times the killer will attend so we will be watching. I don't have the particulars yet, but I'll let you know."

Donna said, "I may know before you."

# Chapter
# 8

Both Lou and Donna took a half day off on Friday to attend Reva's morning services. Lou didn't know the woman, but he was sure Donna would need a lot of support to get through this tough time.

When he picked her up, she was wearing a navy dress with matching high heels. Her long dark hair was pinned up and topped with a small hat. A pearl necklace and earrings finished the classy look. With her beauty and blue eyes, it was enough to make a man drool, and Lou was pretty sure that was precisely what he was doing. He worked hard to keep his feelings for her from showing, but sometimes he couldn't help it.

Lou was the one who loved dressing to the max every day. High-dollar suits were his norm. It was just who he was. Unlike him, Donna only dressed up for rare occasions. Work clothes for her would always be jeans and three-inch heeled ankle-boots. Tops would be tees, sweaters or sweatshirts, with light jackets.

*She's always gorgeous, but today she takes my breath away.* Lou smiled like a love-sick schoolboy and felt like one.

The day was the perfect spring day. The sun was shining, and a light warm breeze kept the birds happily singing. Donna wondered how such a beautiful day could harbor such pain.

The services were held at the Lakeview Funeral Home & Cemetery, one of the best in the county. Donna met some of Reva's family - a couple of her brothers and an older sister. After a while, she couldn't keep count. There were eight siblings in all. Although Reva was not the first one of the siblings to pass away, she was undoubtedly the first to be murdered.

Lou and Donna saw Roger and J.C. there but pretended not to know them. Their co-workers were mingling as mourners, but watching every single person who showed up. A pen on Roger's coat pocket was taking pictures every few seconds.

Lou steered Donna from the viewing room. He knew his partner would fall apart to see her friend lying in a casket.

An hour later, they were outside at the grave site where the services were held.

Donna looked around. It was an attractive area. Lakeview, itself, was on beautiful property. Each grave site seemed to have a lovely view.

With her mind and heart torn over Reva, she didn't remember much about what was said or even who said it, but she did remember walking up to Marvin Rong after the service, and giving him a big hug as they both cried.

When it was over, Lou took Donna to lunch. He chose a nice restaurant so she would be able to relax before going to work.

Not much was said, but Donna was able to get a handle on some of her pain. She knew she would have to before going back to the precinct. The old Donna was trying to emerge. She wanted to be the strong woman Reva had so admired about her.

On the way out the door, Donna hit Lou on his arm. "Thanks for the nice lunch, partner."

Lou grabbed his arm and wailed like he was dying. "Woman, you are trying to kill me! I know you are!"

"Wow. You are smarter than you look!" Donna retorted. Their laughter lifted spirits.

~~~~~

Back at the precinct, wolf whistles followed Donna as she walked up to Roger's desk. The detectives were not used to seeing her all dressed up.

"See anything? Any clues?"

"We took pictures, so we will be going over those this afternoon. Nothing that we can put our fingers on, but maybe the pictures will help." Roger had already seen her dressed up that morning and didn't try to embarrass her.

Donna nodded and returned to her desk. The last of the background reports were in, and they were pouring all of their attention on them.

Lou's phone rang. It was Parry requesting their presence in his office.

"What's up, boss?" Lou quickly sat down so Parry wouldn't get irritated with him. Donna followed.

"You tell me! What have you found out? It has been a week!"

Lou told him of the massive amount of files they had to go through – cases the judge had heard, this time going back five years. He also added the interviews and the background checks. That did not placate Parry.

"Any progress? Any leads? ANYTHING?"

"Chief, I know there hasn't been much progress that can be seen, but each case, each person we eliminate is a step closer to whoever may be responsible for Patricia's disappearance." Donna knew it was true but was just as frustrated as her boss.

"You know as well as we do that she is eighteen years old and can come and go as she pleases. Without a body, we have to assume she is still alive! Granted, finding her purse and the cell phone doesn't look good, but the only benefit of her being kidnapped would be ransom – and there has been no demand.

"She could have ditched her stuff to start a new life somewhere else, as a different person.

We don't know. Nevertheless, right now, it is nothing more than a missing adult." Donna stopped to catch her breath.

"Not good enough! I want some answers. Judge Gattino wants answers! You are right. We don't know if she is alive or dead! Find out! You are two of my best detectives. Now go prove it!"

Both got up and left the office. They knew the files had to be reviewed before they could proceed any further, so back to the paperwork they went.

The only bright spot for the day was the fact they both would have tomorrow off since they worked the Saturday before unless something urgent came in.

Detectives were expected to work every other Saturday and one Sunday a month, unless their case had specific leads, then they could be working night and day.

An exhausted detective wasn't any good to anyone.

~~~~~

Donna was awakened Saturday morning around seven by the phone ringing. It was the precinct.

"Detective Decker, this is Amy Castor."

"Hi, Amy. How are you doing? We haven't talked in a while."

"I'm super. I got a call from the sheriff of Haskell County, Travis Biggs. He wants to talk to you right away, but I wouldn't give him your home number without your permission. It is okay?"

"Amy, give me his number, and I will call him back." After Donna wrote the number down, she thanked Amy for the call. She was grateful her home number wasn't freely given, even to other officers of the law.

After dialing the number, she identified herself and asked for the sheriff.

"This is Sheriff Biggs."

"Sheriff, this is Detective Decker of the Wichita Police Department. I understand you wanted to speak with me."

"Yes, detective. I hear you have a missing girl. Is that right?"

"Yes, it is. Her name is Patricia Gattino. Why, do you have any information?"

"I don't know. I wanted to let you know we have a Jane Doe, who *might* be your missing. About five or six days ago, we discovered a girl hanging from a tree. She left a suicide note, but we have not been able to ID her."

Donna almost choked. "Hung? With a note? Tell me everything you know."

"My deputy found her when we received a call from a farmer out that way. He was devastated to see a girl hanging from a tree. Anyway, we put her in the morgue and then had the local newspapers asking questions about who she might be.

"We even checked with our surrounding counties, but no one had a missing person with her description. Then I decided to hit larger cities and there in Sedgwick, you have a girl missing who just might be our Jane Doe."

With her mind racing, she had two important questions for him. The first was, "What does she look like?"

"I can fax her photo to you if you like."

"No. I am not in my office. Text it to me. What did the suicide note say?" Donna held her breath not really wanting to hear the words.

"It said, 'If I can't have my Daddy, then I don't want to live.' Don't know what that means, but it is pretty sad. Sounds like her old man died or something."

Donna's phone tinged, and she knew the text had come in. She flipped over to the incoming and stared at the photo of a dead girl. A dead girl who looked just like Patricia Gattino.

It took a moment for Donna to get her voice back. "That looks like our girl, sheriff. She will need to be transported to our morgue, as you know. Plus, my partner and I will have to come out to you so you can show us where you found her and anything else you might remember."

"No problem, detective. We will need a personal ID anyway when you can get here. We can't go by photo alone. Sorry about the girl, but it solves your case."

*Solves it? It just escalated it sky high, but no need to go there.*

"Thank you, sheriff, for calling. We will be there this afternoon." Donna hung up and sat still for what seemed like hours, but in truth was only minutes.

*Pat was found hung. Like the girl in Butler County. With the same note. What. Is. Going. On?*

She called Lou and told him about the conversation with Travis Biggs. She also told him to pack for a possible overnight trip. They were going to Sublette, Kansas, county seat for Haskell.

Donna then called Parry.

# Chapter 9

"What's happening? What am I going to tell the judge?"

"Please, chief, don't tell him anything, yet. Let's get her body back here first. There is a chance it isn't her. *Small*, but you don't want to put the parents through this until we know for sure.

"Plus, I need you to send a van out to retrieve the body and bring it back. Lou and I are going out to look at the scene where she was found. We may be gone all weekend, but we'll keep in touch."

Parry sighed but agreed. "Okay, I won't say a word for now. Go and find out what you can. I'm off tomorrow so call my cell."

They said their goodbyes and Donna packed a small bag to get her through a couple of days if needed.

Within an hour Lou arrived, and she jumped into his Mercedes to head west. The 200-mile trip would take about three and a half hours, but that could be a good thing. Getting their head around this might take that long.

Lou was the first to start in. "Are you serious? Hung? Like the El Dorado girl? Why?"

"I don't have any answers, that's for sure. Is this a new 'teen' suicide fad like in the 80's?" Donna was thinking about the thousands of teenagers that 'followed' the fashion of killing themselves by fad.

Then there are the 'death groups' on the 'net that actually *encourage* teens to kill themselves! Those sickos alone have been the cause of tens-of-thousands of teen suicides a year, around the world. So far, no country has been able to prosecute them.

"I have to tell you, Lou. I am not sure how to handle this one."

After talking through each and every step of the investigation for two hours, Donna closed her eyes and fell asleep. Lou would look over at her as he drove on to Sublette.

*She is so beautiful. So perfect. At least, perfect for me. What am I going to do about her? If I say anything, she will hate me forever, and certainly not want me to be her partner. But I don't think I could go on being a detective if she wasn't my partner. Think? I know I couldn't.*

Lou knew he was in a lot of trouble over his feelings for Donna, but he didn't have a clue what to do about it. For now, there wasn't a thing he *could* do.

As they were driving into Sublette, he reached over to gently shake Donna awake. She sat up and brushed her hair, smiling sheepishly. It was hard for her to stay awake when in a moving vehicle for long periods of time. That's just the way she was.

First stop would be to meet the sheriff. They parked at 300 S. Inman St. and went in. Sheriff Biggs was waiting for them.

"Glad to see you, folks. First, we will go to the morgue so you can see the body yourselves. Hopefully, we can get an identification, finally. I have been told the van from Wichita to pick up the body will be here in about an hour or so. If it is not your lady, I will have to send them back empty.

At the morgue, neither one of them was anxious to see if it was their missing girl. They knew what Patricia looked like from her senior picture, and those shown to them by her father.

They both took a deep breath as the coroner opened the drawer. When it was all pulled out, he uncovered her face.

It was Patricia Gattino. No doubt about it. Just like the photo the sheriff sent.

Donna nodded at the sheriff.

Biggs turned to the coroner, "Prepare the body for transport to Wichita. They will pick her up shortly. She is no longer a Jane Doe. Her name is Patricia Gattino."

Donna knew that meant this body was no longer the sheriff's problem. It was theirs.

"Doctor, was there any sign of foul play? Anything that didn't look right?" Donna needed to make sure.

"No. I didn't find anything out of the norm. Hanging from a rope around the neck is what killed her. Sad, too. A girl dying this young. Why would she want to end her life? And what's with this father thing?"

"We don't know for sure." Lou was glad Parry was going to be the one to break the news to Judge Gattino. What a mess.

When they left the building, they were directed to the sheriff's SUV. Being so tall, Lou preferred the front seat where he could move it back for more leg room, so Donna slipped into the back.

As Sheriff Biggs drove out of town, Lou asked how far away she was found.

"Actually only about ten miles. Not far from town, but just far enough to not be found immediately. Doc says she was probably dead about twelve hours when we found her. That might be why she picked this spot."

Donna jumped on that one. "But we are not aware that she had ever been to Sublette, let alone knew the area. But, as you say, she could have just gone out far enough she thought would cover her tracks. Who knows what this girl was thinking."

Within minutes, the sheriff pulled the car off the road. They were out in the country with farmland on both sides of a small two-lane road. The road was paved, but it was apparent there was little traffic.

The soft wind was blowing the tree limbs that lined the fences. On any other day, this would be an excellent place to sit and have a picnic. Country, peace, quiet, light breeze...

*Is this why she picked this place? Peace and quiet? Unlike city life?* Donna was trying hard to put the pieces together, but she only came up with more questions.

"Here is the tree she used." Sheriff Biggs pointed out a sturdy limb that was rising high over the fence to about ten feet in the air.

"You can see she got over this old fence pretty easy, then just climbed up this big limb until she was out as far as she wanted to go... tied one end to the tree, put the other around her neck, and jumped off. That would sure do it. Sad." He shook his head. None of them understood why a person would do that to themselves.

A close look at the old fence made it clear someone had crushed the top down so you could just step over it.

The 'branch' the sheriff spoke of, was a separate tree growing out of the base of another tree. It was about fifteen-inches in diameter and started from the ground up. It would have been easy to climb that tree trunk as it curved high over the fence to the road.

UNHOLY REVENGE

Donna spent the next ten minutes taking pictures of every inch of the area. Yes, the police had been all over the place and that probably ruined any chance of getting the tiniest clue, but she wanted them… no, she *needed* them for herself. Donna was having a tough time accepting this suicide.

After driving back into town, Sheriff Biggs accepted Lou's offer for coffee.

Sitting around a table at a diner, the sheriff was obviously sad.

"We don't see things like this around here. Couldn't believe it. Didn't want to believe it. A pretty young thing like that just up and decides life is not worth living anymore."

Lou and Donna brought him up to date on her background and family history.

"A judge! Dear God in Heaven! What he must be going through now." Pulling a piece of paper out of this pocket, he handed it to Donna. "This is the suicide note. I knew you would want it."

Biggs received a text the body had been picked up, so he passed the news on. Lou and Donna decided it was time to go home. Everything they came for had been accomplished so they didn't need to stay the night. The detectives said their goodbyes to the sheriff and left Sublette.

Donna got on her cell and called Parry. She set up a meeting with him for ten in the morning in his office. They all were supposed to have Sunday off, but she didn't see how that was going to happen.

"Meeting? What is that all about?" Lou was at a loss.

"Lou, we originally thought this might be something like a fad for teens, but I am just not feeling it. Pat was eighteen, not exactly a fourteen-year-old hormonal and emotional wreck. She was graduating from high school and already enrolled in college for the fall. Not exactly a girl who was thinking of killing herself. Something about the notes, too, has me reeling."

"So what are you thinking, woman?"

"What I'm thinking is both of our suicides were murders."

~~~~~

It was a beautiful Sunday morning. Parry would be waiting for them in his office. When they got there, Homicide Division was buzzing as Lou and Donna got off the elevator.

"Hey, I thought you guys had the day off!" It was Dale.

Lou waved and said, "We only wish."

They each grabbed a cup of coffee from the break room and went into Parry's office. Once the door was shut and they were all seated, it was Parry who spoke first.

"Okay. None of this is going to be any good, but tell me why you wanted this meeting."

"I wanted to bring you up to date as well as turn things around a bit. I think we have this all wrong." Donna had their attention.

"I'm listening."

"Did you hear about the teen who hung herself in Butler County a little over a week ago?"

"Yes. So?"

"So, Patricia supposedly hung herself and left the same note. It said the same thing. 'If I can't have my Daddy, I don't want to live.' When we heard about Alani, Lou and I accepted the suicide everyone else thought it was. But with Pat having the same M.O., I just don't believe it.

"Chief, I would bet my badge that they were both murdered." Donna didn't have to wait long for his response.

"What? In Butler County, they said it was 'obviously' a suicide!"

"I believe the killer made it look that way. Before you go telling Judge Gattino that his daughter killed herself over him, I think we need a little more time."

"Detective, we don't have any more time. The media will be all over this!"

"What I am trying to say is, you can tell the judge about his only child being gone. I understand that. But don't tell him the means of death or any details *just* yet. Don't put him through that anguish. Give us until tomorrow morning to look into this further."

Donna let out a deep sigh, "Like I said, I would bet my badge this is a murder."

Parry glared at her. "You just may be doing that."

# Chapter 10

Donna was willing to take that chance.

"Lou and I will go to El Dorado and speak with Deputy Wallace. We will go over everything with him to see if there is any connection between the two girls. I truly believe they were murdered by the same person."

Lou and Donna sat quietly, watching Parry stare at his desk. It was apparent his thoughts were turning over everything Donna had said, repeatedly.

After several minutes, he looked up and said, "Okay. But just until morning."

They got up to leave, and Parry added one last thought. "I hope your right. I don't want to tell my friend his daughter killed herself."

They quietly shut the door and left the building.

While Lou was driving to El Dorado, Donna called the Butler County Sheriff's Office located in that city.

After identifying herself, she asked to speak with Deputy Sterling Wallace.

"One moment, please. I'll see if he is in."

Donna was on hold for several minutes and was about to hang up when she heard, "Deputy Wallace."

"Deputy, this is Detective Donna Decker from Wichita. My partner, Lou McGregor and I are on our way to El Dorado and would like to speak with you if we could."

"What's this about, Detective? I am not aware that the case I am working crosses county lines."

"It's about your daughter. It's important we talk."

"I... Uh... I don't want to talk about..."

"Sterling," Donna decided to get personal to reach this poor man. "It is important, and I know you will want to hear what we have to say."

"Um, okay. Meet you here at the precinct." He hung up.

Turning to Lou, she said, "I hope he's still there when we arrive because he was *not* happy about meeting with us."

Within thirty minutes, they parked at the sheriff's office. Once inside, they were told what floor to find Wallace on.

Once there, Sterling Wallace introduced himself. He was a medium skinned black man who looked like he hadn't slept in a month. Donna felt this man was probably attractive when he didn't have that fatigue and pain all over his face.

With him was his young, red-headed partner, Lucas Cameron, who looked to be about thirty or so. Sterling asked if it was okay for his partner to join them.

"He has been a big support for me during all this, and I will probably need him again today."

Lou and Donna didn't mind at all.

They were shown into an interrogation room, where the four sat down.

Lucas stated, "I just want you to know, I am here to listen and be supportive. This is a tough subject for any father to have to go through." He turned his sympathy look to his friend, Sterling.

Sterling's voice was soft and low. "What can you possibly tell me about my daughter that I don't know?"

"We are sorry for your loss and know you must be in such agony over it. It has only been a week, and I am quite surprised that you are back to work so soon." Donna observed his eyes. She didn't want to push him too far.

"I was off a week. Work is better than home at this point. It just reminds me she isn't there. Now, what is this about?"

Lou dropped the bombshell.

"Sterling, another girl has been found hung from a tree – with the identical suicide note."

'What? What are you talking about? Some idiots are out there copy-catting a suicide? What is happening in this world!"

He turned to look at Lucas, who was equally shocked.

"No. No, that is not what we are telling you. We are telling you we think your daughter was murdered."

Sterling sat still and just stared at them. Lou and Donna let him deal with it in his own way.

When he spoke, his voice was low again. "Murdered. Why would you think that?"

Lucas whispered, "Holy Mary, Mother of God…"

Lou jumped in, "Think about it, Sterling! Did you have any problems with Alani? Did she ever complain about you not being around enough? Anything?

"No. Never. I just don't understand…"

"That's our point. She did not kill herself over you. Someone did it for her!"

"The other young lady was eighteen years old. She was enrolled in college in the fall. She was excited about going! We don't believe she killed herself either. She was murdered.

Donna went on, "What we need to find out from you is if there was any connection between these two girls. Why would someone pick these two? There has to be a reason.

"The other girl's name was Patricia Gattino, the daughter of Judge Gattino, of Wichita. Her body was found in Haskell County, out west. Outside of Sublette, actually."

"Detective, I don't know this girl, and I have never been to Sublette in my life. I still don't get the connection. I mean, I am very sorry for the judge's loss, but I don't know what that has to do with me.

"I don't see how they could possibly have known each other. They were far apart in age, and never went to the same school together.

They would never have been in the same summer camp or the likes. I just don't see it."

The three of them talked for a good hour, and Sterling didn't think their thoughts were right. His daughter had killed herself, and that was that.

"I am just going to have to deal with it." Sterling was visibly upset.

Lou left the room and brought back four coffees. They needed something to keep them going.

After a few minutes, Lou's mind hit another thought. "Hey, wait a minute. What if this isn't about the girls at all?"

He turned to Donna and said, "What if this is about Sterling and the judge? The girls were just a way of getting to *them?*"

Donna's eyes got big, and her mind started to whirl.

"Stop right there, guys," Sterling was shaking his head. "Before you go there, I have to tell you, I not only have never met this judge, but I hardly run in the same social circles that he does. We have nothing in common except we have each lost a daughter."

"Let it go, guys. I have to get back to work. Sorry this didn't work out. I would surely like to know my little girl didn't do that to herself, but she did."

Sadly, they saw he was through talking. They packed up their notepads, said their goodbyes to Sterling and Lucas and left.

Sterling Wallace walked with them to the main street door.

"Sorry you made this trip for nothing, Detectives, but I appreciate what you were trying to do. It certainly would help to know... Well, you know... Have a safe trip home." With that, Sterling went back to the elevator and disappeared.

It was late afternoon, so they decided to get something to eat before leaving town. They pulled into a Sonic Drive-in. As they ate, they discussed how the two men could possibly be connected.

"Maybe we are wrong about the men. Maybe it is their wives who connect…? Or their accountants, or their Pastors, or their… Lord, help me." Lou was ready to go anywhere that might find an answer.

He believed as Donna did. The girls were murdered. Something, or someone, connected them. But what?

"I dread to tell Parry we didn't have a 'murder' leg to stand on. And I hate the idea of him telling the judge Pat killed herself when I don't think she did! What I'm saying is, I don't want to see Judge Gattino going through what Sterling is going through." Donna was frustrated.

Lou finished his food and put the trash in the bag. "I know. I feel the same, but we can't prove anything but suicide right now…"

The drive home was quiet. Lou dropped Donna off to pick up her car, and they both headed home. So much for the weekend off.

Donna went to bed early but found sleep not easy to come by. What was she missing? Or wasn't seeing? She usually is good at these kinds of puzzles, but this one was getting to her.

She is sure they were murdered. Now if she could just prove it.

~~~~~

Monday morning found them both not looking forward to facing Parry. He wanted answers this morning that they just didn't have.

Believing the girls were murdered and proving it, are definitely two different things.

Lou's phone rang.

"Detective McGregor."

He immediately heard Lucas yell, "Alani didn't kill herself! She was murdered!"

Lou was brought to silence. He snapped his finger at Donna to pick up her phone and mouthed 'Lucas.' She did and said hello so he would know she could hear also.

"You were right!" Lucas shouted. "It *is* about the judge and Sterling!

"And I *know* who the murderer is!"

# Chapter 11

"Get back here. Right now! I have all the paperwork for you to see! Now! I'm telling you, get here NOW!" With that Lucas hung up.

Lou grabbed his jacket from the back of his chair. Donna had her notepad in hand, and they were running for the elevator.

"MCGREGOR, DECKER! IN MY OFFICE!"

Lou yelled over his shoulder, "Not now, boss. This is important!"

While in the elevator, he looked at Donna and said, "I hope this *is* important or I might not have a job tomorrow."

"Both of us won't." She had no idea what this was about, but she wanted to hear every word.

The trip to El Dorado went fast. Lou put his red light on top and turned on the siren. Getting there was a priority. Donna called Parry and explained their swift departure. When she told him the Butler County Deputy Sheriff claimed to know the killer, their boss understood their sudden disappearance.

Arriving back at the Butler County Sheriff's office found them both hardly able to breathe. What were they about to find out? The Lord only knows.

Lucas was waiting for them. He hurried them into an interrogation room to sit down. There were files and paperwork scattered all over the table.

"Sterling took the day off. Seems his wife is falling apart. I can hardly blame her. I explained to the sheriff what I came up with and he has given me today to take care of this, so we have all the time we need.

"First, is this paperwork… "

He picked up a large file and tossed it in front of them. Donna quickly opened it and viewed it as fast as she could.

It was about a man who was convicted of rape and murder over twenty years ago. *What does this have to do with anything?*

"Okay," Donna said, "I see this is about a man who got what he deserved…"

Lucas jumped in, "Okay. The only way this is going to make any sense is to start from the very beginning. Bear with me as it tends to be a very long story.

"About twenty-five or six years ago, a woman named Blanche, walked out on her husband and little girl. She apparently ran off with some other man. At that time, they lived outside of Derby, in a run-down house on twenty acres.

"The husband, his name was Erick, didn't take his wife leaving very well. He started drinking a lot and doing some drugs. He finally got fired from his job for showing up late, or not at all. That left him and his daughter living on welfare, while the drugs and booze took what little of his mind he had left.

"The little girl was Dana. She was about ten when her mother left. You can imagine how hard that was on her. Plus Erick was drunk most of the time, so she was left to her own devices to grow up.

"Her best friend since grade school was Betsy. They did everything together, and Dana ate and slept over at her friend's house a lot during this bad time in her life."

"Yes, it's a sad story, but what…" Lou was getting a little restless. Donna, on the other hand, was very interested.

"Just wait, just wait. It will all become clear. I told you this is a long story. Be patient. You will be glad you know everything, in the end, I promise you."

Lou nodded.

"Anyway, in Erick's drunkenness and delirium, he started imagining things like someone talking to him. He convinced himself the crazy talk in his head was God… telling him to do things. He really seemed to believe this.

"Okay, so, as the story goes, one day he was actually semi-sober and thought of his daughter, Dana. He drove to the school to pick her up; the first time in weeks. While he was parked there, he saw her best friend, Betsy, hiding around a corner with a boy. They were kissing and apparently, the way he tells it, the boy's hand was under her blouse, feeling her breasts.

"He was outraged! This girl was apparently having sex. To him, that meant she was a whore. He didn't even stay to pick up Dana. He drove back home and drank himself into a stupor over it.

"Erick said God started talking to him about Betsy. He said God told him if he didn't do something about this, then his own daughter would follow in this girl's footsteps and also become a whore.

"Not knowing what to do, God told him he had to show Betsy the error of her ways and then kill her, so he, God, could send her straight to hell."

Donna couldn't help but jump in with, "Oh, my Lord! What in the world…?"

"I know, right? Now, you and I know this is bullshit, but, apparently, this whacko believed it!

"Anyway, so he follows Betsy to a grocery store one weekend. When she exits, he tells her

Dana wanted her to come by the house on her way home. She said okay and got into his car.

"He took her somewhere and raped her repeatedly. That, supposedly, was showing her 'the error of her ways.' And then he strangled her to death.

"Betsy's body was then dumped by the side of the road, just south of Wichita.

"It didn't take long at all to discover the killer was Erick because he was seen picking her up, and he even admitted it. He told everyone what God said and why he had to do it. He really believed what he did was okay because it came from God!

"It took a couple of years to go to trial, but during that time, another tragedy happened.

"About nine months after he was put in jail, his now thirteen-year-old daughter, Dana, was found hung from a tree in their backyard."

Lou and Donna both gasped. They certainly didn't see that coming!

"Yeah. It really rocked the community at the time. She left a long note saying how she hated her father and that he was crazy. She went on and on about how he had ruined her life and took away her best friend. But her main worry seemed to be the future.

"She said she would never be able to have any children because she would be afraid they would turn out like Erick. She felt the only way to stop his psycho madness was to end the genes right here. So she hung herself. No dispute. It was suicide.

"From everything that I have been able to gather, and believe me I was here very late last night when he was told about his daughter, and *given* her suicide note, he denied it. He said she didn't write that note, that she was in despair over losing her loving father – one that would *kill* to protect her! That is the only reason she didn't want to go on living.

"Anyway, after a year or so later, he went to trial and was found guilty. It wasn't hard, because he admitted it, describing every horrible detail. Years later when his attorney filed appeals, DNA was also used to prove it was him, and the motions were denied.

"He was given twenty-to-life here at the El Dorado Correctional Facility. As you know, it is a maximum security prison where only the worst offenders go.

"Currently there is the BTK killer, Dennis Rader, and the filthy Carr brothers. How they got their death sentence overturned to life, I don't know. They certainly don't deserve to live."

Donna spoke up, "Okay, we have this sad story from long ago. But how…"

"I'm getting there. Here's where my partner comes in. He has worked for the Sheriff's office for about a year and a half now. Before that, he was a guard at that prison, and had worked there for about twelve years!

"So he knew this guy?" Lou was becoming interested in what Lucas had to say.

"Sort of. No one 'knows' the inmates, but he was around Erick's cell from time to time. Now, this next part I got from Sterling himself. We were out having a few beers one night because we had the next day off. He was telling me some stories about his time at the prison. And this is one of them.

"A couple of years ago, Sterling was in Erick's section for about a month. As with some of the other inmates, he looked up Erick's crime. Sterling figured if he knew what they were in for, he would know better what kind of person he was up against. Who knows.

"Anyway, he studied up on Erick and his crime. He was utterly disgusted with what the guy had done since he had a little girl himself. In fact, he hated him.

"So, one day Erick asked Sterling if he had a daughter, and he said he did. Well, apparently

Erick was telling him to protect her and don't let any of her friends influence her to be a whore, etc. etc.

"Being a bit defensive, Sterling said something like 'What do you know about protecting your daughter? She killed herself because she couldn't stand being a part of you!' From what Sterling said, Erick came unglued and tried to grab him through the bars. Erick screamed the suicide note was phony and that she loved her Daddy.

"The hate on his face stayed with Sterling for days. He said he left that job a few months later and came here. He was offered more money and fewer hours. Who wouldn't want that?

"Anyway, the most interesting part is, after serving his twenty years, he was let out on parole last month."

Lucas became quiet and looked at them. Lou and Donna stared back.

"Okay. This piece of crap doesn't like Sterling, and I'm sorry he is out. So?" Lou's eyebrows were raised.

Donna finished taking notes and said, "How does this figure into our case?"

"Don't you understand? Remember what Sterling said about the judge and him yesterday? 'We have nothing in common except we have each lost a daughter.' After you left, that thought wouldn't leave my head.

"Sterling went home, but I couldn't let it go. I went over and over it. Yes, the one thing Sterling and the judge has in common is they have lost a daughter!

"*THAT* is the key! That is the connection between them. They have each lost a daughter. Now, who else has lost a daughter that would want to make Sterling pay in the same way?

"Erick hated him for saying his daughter despised her father! It also explains the note – all about missing *Daddy*! Sterling never could understand that with Alani. She only called him Dad. This is it! It's him! Erick Xavier Jefferson killed Alani and the other girl." He pointed to the file.

"Oh, and if you need any more evidence that I am right? Judge Gattino was the presiding judge in Erick's trial."

# Chapter
# 12

"WHAT?" Donna jumped up out of her seat, knocking the chair over. "Judge Gattino? No way!"

"Holy cow," sputtered Lou. "You're right, Lucas. It has to be him! Where is he? How do we find him?"

"I have a call in for his parole officer. I don't have his current address, yet. Before he was arrested, his home was in the country outside of

Derby. A real dive on twenty acres, I think. Of course, that was foreclosed on when he went to jail. Anyway, we know he didn't go back there because it was torn down years ago." Lucas smiled at their amazed faces.

Donna said, "I knew they were murdered. I just had a gut feeling, but I couldn't put it together. You did an awesome job, my friend, and I thank you beyond words."

Coming from such a beautiful woman, Lucas blushed, "It really wasn't me. It's what Sterling said about what he and the judge could possibly have in common that turned the light bulb on. 'Daughters' is the answer."

"And, as it stands, this is a case that involves both Butler and Sedgwick counties, so we will probably run into each other again. At least I would appreciate your keeping us posted on any new info."

Lou was the first to shake his hand. "You can bet on it, Lucas. We owe you big time!"

"Now, I am going to go to my partner's house and explain to him as well as the rest of his family that his daughter did not kill herself. It won't bring Alani back, but at least Sterling won't feel the pain and guilt the note left on him. Have a safe trip back."

They picked up all of the paperwork and laid it in the box Lucas gave them. Now to get back to Wichita and show it all to Parry.

The drive back was both silent and crazy. One moment they were talking over each other about something Lucas said, and then they were both silent. Before they knew it, they were back at the precinct.

~~~~~

They went straight into Parry's office and shut the door.

They spent the next hour showing him the previous crime. They were surprised at how patient he was while they took turns explaining each detail.

Tagged "The God Case" back when it was going to trial, Erick Jefferson still maintained he didn't have a choice. God told him to do it. Those that didn't believe in God said it was a rouse, and those that did believe said God would never do that to an child. Of course, Jefferson said there was nothing innocent about her. Some even called him 'God's Revenger.'

"I remember 'The God Case.' It was a media frenzy back in the 90s." Parry was shaking his head, almost in disbelief.

Donna then told about the conflict Sterling had with Erick, while Sterling was still a prison guard. Even though it was approximately a year before his release, Erick never forgot the humiliation Sterling put him through over his daughter suicide note.

"Obviously, this is the first thing he did when he got out of jail. During their conversations,

Erick knew there was a daughter, and they lived in El Dorado. He found out where Sterling lived, maybe by following him home.

"He followed the daughter until he could kidnap and kill her. Then he was able to leave the note Erick swears is the real note writtn by his daughter when she hung herself.

"His plan was then to get back at the judge who found him guilty all those years ago. No one believed him about God telling him to commit the crime, which he obviously still believes, so he is after revenge. Maybe he even thinks God is telling him to do it. Who knows?" Donna poured it all out.

Parry finally spoke up, "This is incredible. How did you know this?" He was shocked by all they had shown him.

Lou, who was always proud of his partner, said, "It was Donna who knew in her gut it was murder. She's amazing that way, Chief."

Donna jumped in with, "But it was Lucas who was able to put it together so it made sense. Without him, I would still be saying it was murder, but couldn't prove it.He spent a lot of hours researching and putting all this together. Then add the hours it took him to convey the info to us. Sterling couldn't ask for a better partner.

"We would be working on the judge's past cases for months, if not years, before we got back over twenty years ago when Jefferson was convicted!" Donna was still amazed.

"Okay, I want a warrant and APB put out for him. Get information out to all the mid-western states, in case he leaves Kansas. I want every newspaper running his picture. I want every cop to know of him. We have to find this ass!"

"On it, Chief!" Lou and Donna were glad to comply. An All-Points Bulletin would make sure everyone was looking for him.

Lou continued, "And we can be pretty sure about the description of the car we got from that high school girl, is what he is driving!"

Parry stood. "I have to say 'good job,' guys. No matter how it was done, this is a fantastic discovery. Good job.

"Since you guys worked all weekend, take a day off sometime this week and get some rest. Just give me a little heads up. The police will be looking for our killer now.

"As for me, I have to drive out to see my old friend, and tell him his daughter was murdered." Parry didn't look too happy about it. "At least it wasn't suicide."

~~~~~

By the following morning, the story was on the front page of most newspapers around the state, as well as the talk of Kansas television stations. It seems the public couldn't hear enough about this psychopath out for revenge. One newspaper even called it the 'return of God's Revenger.'

Lou and Donna made an appointment to speak with the Prisoner Review Board that set the man free over a month ago. They were granted a meeting the next day as the board would be in Sedgwick County for the week.

Lou started out with, " I am sure you have read the papers or heard the news about Erick Jefferson and the latest murders he has committed. We are not blaming you for releasing Jefferson. We want to make that clear.

"We just need as much information about this man as we can get. The more we know, the easier to catch him. What was it about Erick Jefferson that made you feel he was ready to return to society?"

"First, he recanted his 'excuse' for the killing as being told to do it by God. He took full responsibility for his actions. A vast difference from his trial." The lady was noticeably upset with all that has occurred over their decision.

"He was very adamant that it was the booze and drugs that caused him to hallucinate into thinking God was talking to him. He said he didn't even want to do the crime, but felt God would kill him, or his daughter, if he didn't. But being clean and sober has shown him it was all in his head. Even under the influence of drugs and booze, his not wanting to do the crime showed he wasn't the type of person thinking about killing people.

"He went on to say how very sorry he was for what had happened to that girl he had killed. He told us he had berated himself for twenty years over her not having her life to live. Jefferson didn't mention it, but we all knew he would obviously still have a daughter if he had not done this heinous crime."

One of the gentlemen spoke up, "We didn't take every word he said for the truth, mind you. Several times over the years, he was written up for screaming from his cell about God and what

God wanted him to do to everyone. I figured he was lying to us, so I brought that up to dispute his comment. But, he had a reasonable answer for that, too.

"Jefferson said he continued to play that game in prison to keep the other inmates from bothering him. I felt it was a logical answer. It's hardly the strangest thing that inmates do to stay safe."

They all nodded.

A third said, "He had not caused any other problems in prison for the past twenty years. No fights, no trouble. As he told us, he has been clean and sober for all that time and felt he was able to be a productive member of society again.

"I think we've all seen or known someone who was hooked on something and then came clean. They are two different people. That is what we believed we saw here. A man totally saddened over his crime after he was sober."

The first woman spoke up again, "We all felt he had paid for his crime, was adequately remorseful and was no longer a threat. He met all the criteria to be paroled, so that's what we did.

"Now you tell us he has committed two more murders in less than a month of being free. This is beyond horrible! It is obvious, his recanting of God speaking to him was a lie. What a psycho! Needless to say, his parole was revoked this morning."

The detectives assured them everything that could possibly be done to catch Jefferson was being done. They thanked the board for their time and left.

Lou muttered all the way back to their office. "Did you hear her? 'His parole was revoked...' Like he cares! Erick is getting revenge, his holy revenge against good people.

"It's not holy revenge, Lou. It's as unholy as it gets."

"Unholy Revenge... You are so right."

# Chapter
# 13

"Hey, Lou." It was J.C. "I have a 'thing' I have to do tomorrow evening, and I really don't want to go alone."

Lou liked J.C. and said, "When? What's up?"

"Okay. Remember I told you about Mary Louise Quinton, the girl trying to get away from her pimp? That's how I got this scar?"

"Sure. She's now a school teacher, you said." Lou grinned. Great ending to a great story.

"Yeah, well, she called me at home last night. It seems her boyfriend has asked her to marry him. She says she is in love with him, but he doesn't know about her past. Mary said she just couldn't get the words out.

"So, she asked me to come over and explain it all to him. If he still wants to marry her after finding out the truth, then she will say 'yes' to him. But the only time this week that they have an evening free is tomorrow.

"Anyway, Roger has a family thing planned for Wednesday evening, so I would be grateful if you could accompany me."

"Sure. I don't have a problem with that. I hope he is not a jerk and leaves her over it." Lou shook J.C.'s hand. "Remind me tomorrow afternoon, okay?"

"Sure will. Roger and I are working this evening. Feel sorry for us, okay? We will be at the dental clinic where the Walters woman worked. After everyone gets off work, they have agreed to stay so we can ask questions and show photos. Would you like to come along?" J. C. was smirking.

"You know, I have to mop floors tonight. Otherwise, I would love to, but I just can't!" Both laughed at the joke.

~~~~~

When Roger and J.C. got ready to leave that evening, they said their goodbyes to Lou and Donna. Hopefully, they would be able to get some clues from the employees of the clinic.

They talked as they drove to the far east side of town. Little had been found out about Walter's killer, and Parry was getting on them.

After getting all of the funeral photos blown up to 8 x 10s, they had a box full to show around.

The pictures were a long shot, but right now, it is the only one they had.

Once there, they knocked on the already locked door. Dr. Rong let them in, then closed the curtain over the doors and windows.

In the waiting room was about fifteen employees and the four dentists who worked there.

"Thank you very much for agreeing to stay late tonight to talk with us. It really is more convenient for us to come here than to have all of you go downtown, right?" Roger joined in the laughter. "Yeah, that's what I thought.

"First, if anyone has any idea who may have wanted to hurt Reva, write it down and bring it to us. In the meantime, we are going to start passing around pictures that were taken at her funeral. You never know who will show up. Take a close look. Check out everything in each picture. If you see *anything* that is wrong or out of place or *anyone* who shouldn't be there, let us know!"

J.C. grabbed a large handful and started them on the left side of the group and had them passed around. It was slow going, but the detectives were glad everyone was taking the time to look closely.

As the photos started moving toward the back, and then to the right side of the group, J.C. handed out more photos to the left. The group was quiet and not a word was said.

It went this way for about twenty-five minutes, when a girl in the back yelled, "IT CAN'T BE!"

Roger, who felt half asleep by this time jumped up and walked toward her. He had a glimmer of hope in him.

"What is it? What's your name?"

"Jeni. This photo! See that guy way back there. That's the guy Reva threw out of the office, two or three weeks ago?"

One of the other girls said, "Let me see that again." She looked at it and shook her head. "Doesn't look like anyone I have seen here before."

"I did. Really. This guy came here all drugged up, hardly able to walk. Apparently, it was the second time it had happened.

"Reva came out here into the waiting room and told him to leave and never return. Since this had happened before, she said he was not to come back again, ever. He was to find another dentist because Dr. Rong would not see him again!

"She had to physically turn him around and push him outside. 'Don't come back,' she said. 'You are no longer welcome here.' All of the people in the waiting room stood up and applauded her when she came back in. She just smiled and went back to work.

"I mean, I had only worked here about ten days, but I was astonished at how brave she was. He wasn't very big, but it could have gotten ugly."

Roger took the picture, "Okay everyone, I want each one of you to look at this picture and see if you recognize this man. We need a name."

The picture was sent back around the group. In the meantime, J.C. went through all the remaining images trying to find any others that had the same man in it, but there were none. They only had that one to go on.

"I just don't see it."

"He doesn't look familiar to me."

"I remember Reva kicking a guy out, but that was months ago, wasn't it? And it wasn't him."

No one could identify the guy. Only Jeni, a newcomer, thought it was him. When everyone else denied the photo, she became unsure.

"Maybe I'm wrong. I… I know I haven't been here long… I…"

"Don't you worry about a thing. We appreciate your input and thank you for letting us know." Roger was also doubtful at this point.

After the excitement settled down, all of the rest of the photos were sent around. None of them received a comment.

After two hours, they packed the photos back up and thanked everyone for their time and help. With that, they left.

Driving away, Roger asked J.C., "What do you think?"

"I sure felt sorry for Jeni. She's new and doesn't know the clients as well as the others. It was an honest mistake."

"Yeah, I think so, too. Boy, for a moment there, I thought we were getting lucky! There went our last hope of generating any clues. Any brilliant ideas on where to go now?"

"Yeah. To get something to eat."

"Okay, that will give us some quiet time to go over everything... again. I already told my wife I would be having dinner with you."

Roger pulled into the Towne East Mall and went to the Longhorn Steak House. J.C. immediately approved.

"Hey, if we have to work, might as well eat well!"

Once seated, they looked the menu over and ordered. While waiting for their meals, they discussed what they knew.

"Okay, She was viciously murdered in her own car. Blood everywhere. The killer had to be soaked in it himself."

"Yes, but remember, it was at night after she got off of work. He could have walked along in the dark and no one notice he is covered in blood... What do you think?"

Roger, shook his head. "Possible, but she got off before it was dark. Now, she might have gone shopping or, say, went to mail a package, something like that, which would have made her out on the south Webb Road area in the dark. Not impossible, but we can't confirm that."

"Okay, could he have abducted her earlier and had her to drive that way?"

"Yep. Seems likely, even. But her daughter didn't know that she was going to do anything after work. Normally Reva would tell her daughter so she wouldn't worry about her. However, it could have been a last minute thing..."

Their dinners were delivered, and they were too busy eating to talk.

# Chapter
# 14

Wednesday, Donna took her day off to do some shopping and clean house. Lou spent the day going over more paperwork.

The highlight of his day was when he got the call that Harley Borden, their initial but nasty suspect, had been arrested on multiple drug counts. The narcotics detective said they had enough to send him away for the next twenty years.

Lou texted the info to Donna, who also thought it was a great turn of events.

By the end of the day, J.C. was standing at his desk.

"You ready for this, Lou?"

"As I'll ever be. Let's get going."

They chatted like old friends on the way to Mary's west side home. J.C.'s concern was the same that Lou had mentioned the day before.

"What if he storms out and never wants to speak to her again when he hears she used to be on the street?"

"I hear ya," Lou said, "but there is nothing we can do about that, my friend. Besides, it is better it happened now, than for them to be married, and he walks out on her. Any way you look at it, it isn't easy."

Once there, she answered the door on the first knock. Mary hugged J.C. and invited them in.

Inside, they were introduced to Larry Weldom, Mary's boyfriend. He was charming.

"I have to tell you guys, I am a bit nervous about all this. I mean, I asked the woman of my dreams yesterday if she will marry me and instead of saying yes, she says she wants me to talk to a police detective first! I think you can see where I am coming from! Who does that?" Larry sat back down as they laughed at his comment.

J.C. took over. "I can certainly see your point, Larry, and I don't blame you a bit. I think I would be more than a little nervous! I also want you to know my friend, Lou here, won't be doing much talking. I am the one that has the info you need. He came along because he has nothing else to do, and he's too ugly to get a date."

Everyone laughed as Lou looked at J.C. like he was going to hit him. When the laughter died down, J.C. continued.

"I have Mary's permission to speak honestly and openly about everything. If you have any questions, just stop me and ask. I will be glad to answer them all.

Larry nodded. The men were all seated in the living room area. It was small, and the dining table was only six feet away sitting next to a window. That is where Mary decided to stay while all of this is going on.

"Just so you will know, seven years ago, when I got involved with her life, I was not this incredible, handsome detective you see before you today. I was merely a beat cop out on patrol. Yeah, you can feel sorry for me, later.

"Okay, Larry, I have to assume you don't know anything about Mary's past or her upbringing. Is that right?"

"Yes, except she was born in Kansas and raised here in Wichita. She hasn't talked much about her past." Larry glanced at Mary, who was looking out the window, next to the table.

"Okay, Mary was raised here in Wichita, as you said. However, it wasn't very pretty. Her father didn't want to be a father, so he was never in her life. Her mother, apparently, took that news hard and turned to drugs."

Larry looked with sympathy at Mary, who only looked out the window.

"Now, I have to tell you, Larry, Mary was one great kid. Her mother was using, and using a lot, but Mary stayed away from drugs. She did not want to be like her mother. Oh, Mary didn't blame her mother for what she was doing, but she felt sorry for her because her mother's life was being destroyed by those drugs. She could see that and didn't want it to happen to her. She was one smart girl! She spent all her free time taking care of herself and her mother."

Again Larry looked at Mary, this time with a smile.

"One day when Mary was sixteen, she was kidnapped while she walked home from school. Yes, I can see the horror on your face. It really was bad. You see, the culprit was a low-life pimp. He doesn't deserve a name, so I will just call him a pimp. He filled Mary with drugs until she didn't even know who she was, and sold her to men on the street. They didn't care that she was in a stupor. After all, she was young, and they got what they wanted."

Larry's face was now in his hands. They couldn't see what he may be thinking. Mary was still staring out the window.

"You see, Larry, Mary had no choice in what was happening to her. She was so doped up, she didn't even care anymore. Well, after a couple of years, the pimp decided he didn't need to waste as many drugs on her as before, because she was already used to the life and all. Plus it was drugs he could take himself, or sell for more dollars.

"So he cut back on her drastically, and for the first time since she was kidnapped, Mary understood the world around her. She registered what that pimp had done to her. Obviously this is not the life she had chosen for herself, so she wanted to do something about it. Plus, she was worried about her mom. Who was taking care of her? She was really concerned.

"Larry, for the next nine months, she played his game but watched every move he made, trying to find a way to escape. Then one night, she felt it was her chance. She decided she would rather die than live that way any longer."

Larry's face was still in his hands, but Lou thought he heard him cry.

"So that night, she was supposed to meet her trick at a sleazy motel. The pimp took her there and sat in the parking lot out front waiting for her. Well, she went in and told the guy she was dirty and wanted to take a shower. The dude didn't mind, after all, he wanted her clean, right?

"Well, she turned on the shower and opened the bathroom window and climbed out. Everything would have been fine, except for the fact that the guy heard the window and went out front and told the pimp, cause he wanted his money back.

"So the pimp gets out of the car and runs around to the back and catches Mary just as she was starting to run. She screams as he pulls a knife and threatens to cut her throat."

Larry glanced up with his wet eyes and stared at Mary. He didn't move, he just stared.

J.C. and Lou exchange nervous glances. Both were thinking the same thing. Is this where Larry runs out of her life?

"So, Larry, I happen to be on a beat that night. I heard the screams, so I stop my squad and run into the alley.

"The pimp is so mad at Mary, he doesn't even hear me coming up behind him. I grab him with one arm and shove him down. I grab my gun with the other. Well, he jumps up… more like a spring if you ask me, it was so fast. Anyway, he is in my face with that knife and cuts the gash you see on my forehead. That is when I shot him."

Larry's face went back into his hands.

J.C. continued, "Now, Larry, not only did she risk her life to get away from this dog, but she wasn't through yet. With very little help, she got off the drugs, got completely clean and never touched the stuff again.

"Unfortunately, her mother had already passed away from drug use, during the time Mary was held captive. We can only hope the drugs kept her from knowing what happened to her baby girl.

"Anyway, Mary was still the incredible girl she was before the kidnapping. She got her GED and went to college. She is, as you know, an excellent school teacher, helping those less fortunate make something of their lives.

"In all my years as a cop, shoot, even as a father and husband, I have never met a more wonderful and strong woman as Mary is. When she asked me to come here tonight to explain her terrible situation, I was most honored to. She will always have my highest respect.

"That's it, Larry. The ugly story about her past that she couldn't even explain to the man she is in love with. So what do you think?" J.C. stared at Larry, wondering what would come next.

At this time, Larry's eyes were no longer wet. He looked over at Mary who was still staring out the window. Several moments passed in silence.

Larry slowly got up, walked over to Mary, who finally turned from the window to look at him.

He got down on one knee and said, "Mary, will you do me the honor of being my wife? For what you have gone through, I can't even imagine, but to see you today tells me you are a much better person than I. But I ask you to accept me, as well as my faults and I promise to honor you and cherish you for the rest of my life."

He reached into his pocket and brought out the ring he had tried to get her to wear the day before. She said 'yes' and slipped it on her finger. They stood and hugged each other. Both of them were crying.

When J.C. and Lou left, the happy couple were still holding each other, and it appeared they would never let go.

"Wow." That's all Lou could think to say once they were driving away. "Wow."

"Yeah, I know. Praise the Lord, it worked out. There were a couple of times I was concerned he couldn't handle it."

"You said she had a little help… what did that mean?"

"Oh, she needed a few things to get back on her feet. Nothing big. Things like an apartment, clothes, food, just stuff." J.C. smiled in remembrance.

"Nothing big? Apartment? Clothes? Where did she get the money for that?" Lou was now staring at his friend.

"Oh, I talked it over with my wife, Julie, and we decided we could afford to take a couple of grand out of savings and help her out. We found her a decent apartment. It was small for sure, but in a decent neighborhood – something she never had before. As for clothes, all she had was the clothes she wore that night I found her.

"Well, Julie took her to Goodwill shopping. I guess they had a ball!. My wife said they laughed for three solid hours while Mary tried on everything there. They bought a ton of clothes, shoes, purses, plus things for the apartment. Mary didn't care a bit the clothes were used. She was just so happy to have normal clothes again!

Julie and Mary are still friends today." J.C. chuckled again at the memories.

"Why you old dog. It is because of you Mary is where she is today!"

"Oh, no! Absolutely not! It's all her! All the apartments and clothes in the world can't make someone do something they don't want to do. Mary wanted to better herself. She wanted a normal life. She wanted it, and she went after it. Nothing I did could force that to happen.

"She did it herself – and after all she had been through! After she got on her feet, Mary even bought a nice cemetery plot for her mother and had her body moved from the county burial spot. I'm telling you, she is an exceptional human being."

Lou didn't say anything more. But, he thought about what a wonderful man J.C. was and how glad he was to have been asked to come tonight. He was in awe of his new friend.

# Chapter
# 15

The next day, Donna was already at her desk when Lou came in. She told him there had been no sightings of Jefferson or his blue car.

"Do you think he left the state?"

Donna replied, "Could be. For that matter, Lou, he could be out of the country by now. Man, I hope not."

J.C. came in and Lou was surprised to see a worried look on his face. It wasn't the happy guy who dropped him off at the precinct last night to pick up his car.

But it reminded him of the time he had and told Donna about it. He was still in awe, and his partner felt it, too.

They had been going over the files from Lucas for about an hour when Roger approached them.

"'Morning, guys. Donna, I thought you might want to know. We may have a name for the guy who killed your friend, Reva."

Donna jumped up out of her chair. "Who is it? How did you find him? Why did he do it?"

Roger laughed. "Settle down, now. We don't have all that info yet. But I'll tell you what I do have. A couple of days ago, we stopped by the clinic after work to talk with all of her co-workers.

We showed everyone pictures taken at the funeral.

"Well, there was this one gal, Jeni, who said she recognized one guy, way in the back of one picture. We couldn't find him in any other images. Jeni hadn't been working there very long, and her co-workers said 'no, it wasn't one of their clients.'

"So, Jeni decided she must be mistaken. To tell you the truth, J.C. and I thought she was, too. After all, no one else recognized him.

"Well, she called me this morning. She said she was right about that guy. I have to tell you, I immediately went on the defensive and thanked her for her efforts, and we would look into it, blah, blah, blah.

"But no, she wasn't through. She said it was a client from the dental clinic, and she could prove it; She found out his name, address, and everything! Wow. *Now* she had my attention!

"Long story short, she couldn't talk as she was at work but would meet with us at lunch today. We picked a nearby McDonalds.

"Donna, I knew you would want to know!" Roger looked excited at this turn of events.

"Want to *know?* I want to go *with* you!"

"Uh, no. I don't think that would be a good idea. We don't want to overwhelm her with cops she doesn't know. I promise. I'll keep you posted."

Donna didn't like it but understood his reasoning. "Okay. Wow. I hope she's right."

Lou jumped in, "Good luck. How's J.C. doing? He looked a little down when he came in this morning."

"I don't know, really. He has been on the phone a lot today. To tell you the truth, I am not sure what is going on."

~~~~~

Roger and J.C. arrived ten minutes before noon, parked, and waited for Jeni to show up at McDonalds. About fifteen minutes later, she drove up and parked her car. They got out and joined her inside.

Jeni was obviously nervous, and Roger wanted to help.

"It's okay, Jeni. You don't have to worry about your boss or anything. We won't tell them anything you say unless we absolutely have to. We just appreciate you wanting to help out."

"I really liked Reva. She had faith in me that I would be good at my job. She said she would help me. None of the others really care about me at all."

"Okay, tell us about this client from your clinic."

"Well, for me at least, he was easy to recognize because he was so, well, unattractive. But I had no idea what his name was. As you know, I'm new. After everyone else denied he was a client, I really believed they were right. That is until yesterday afternoon!" She stopped to drink some coffee.

"You have our attention," J.C. said, "what happened yesterday afternoon?"

Jeni smiled and said, "His mother came in!"

Roger looked a little confused. "You didn't know his name, but you do now because his mother came in? Do I have that right?"

"Yes. You see, his mother looks a lot like him. Not as bad, of course, but they have a lot of similarities. Granted, she is a little plump, and he is a little..."

Roger asked, "What do you mean by 'little?'"

"Uh, well, he was short, about five-six and skinny. Too skinny, but that was probably due to the drugs.

"Anyway, after showing her inside, I went to the computer to check on her. I got her name and address. I then saw her son was also a client because he shows the same address. That is when I knew it was the guy in the photo."

"Okay. We're ready. Who is it?"

"The mother's name is Claire Sullivan, and she lives on E. Skinner Street. Here is the address. Her son lives with her. His name is Jason. He is the one that came in all drugged up, and I saw it!"

"We thank you for your help, Jeni. We will get right on this and see what we can uncover.' The detectives got up to go.

"Good luck, guys. This guy has to pay for what he did to a wonderful person."

The ride back to the precinct was fast, and the first thing they did was run a check on both Claire and Jason.

Claire was a widow and had been for some time. Around fifty-five years old, she was on disability for a car accident that left a leg messed up. Otherwise, not so much as a parking ticket. Her son had been arrested for drug possession and was given probation and community time. He was a college dropout. Other than that, they didn't find any more on him.

"Roger, the guy does have a drug background. Maybe he is the guy Reva threw out all drugged up? Just because he hasn't been caught, doesn't mean he isn't using."

Roger nodded. "I hear ya."

Roger then suggested they pay a visit to the home address and see if he was there. They sure wanted to talk to him. J.C. agreed and thought they might even get a confession!

"Dream on, J.C. That would make our jobs way too easy..." Roger chuckled as they headed for the elevator.

The ride back out east didn't take long. East Skinner is a lower-end neighborhood, mostly small, older houses with one-car garages. When they arrived, they parked at the curb, then knocked on the door.

A stocky woman who appeared to be older than her years answered the door and was frightened when she saw the badges as they identified themselves.

"Uh, what brings you here?" She was surprised but invited them into the small living room. She hobbled on what appeared to be a bad leg in order to sit down.

"Can I get you some coffee, or maybe tea?" Claire was the epitome of a sweet lady.

After declining refreshments, Roger said, "Ma'am, is your son here?"

"Why, no. He isn't. He left town a few days ago. He didn't say where he was going either. Not that he would tell me anything, anyway."

"Does he leave town often without telling you?

"My, he does whatever he wants to do. It has been years since he took any advice from his mother. But, no. He doesn't leave town often." They noticed the sad look on her face.

"Prior to leaving a few days ago, has he been in town? I mean, he has been around for several weeks here?"

"Oh yes, for several months he has been living here with me. I mean, he doesn't have a family of his own, so there was really no reason for him to pay rent for someplace else. You sure you don't want any tea?"

They were sure.

"Can we see his room? Do you mind?"

"Of course not. Come this way. There isn't much left. Looks like he is going to be gone a while."

They went down a small short hallway. It was a two bedroom home, and she showed them to Jason's. It was small and neat.

After looking through the drawers and closet, they discovered hardly anything to show he had been there. He definitely planned on being gone a while. From the looks of it, a long while!

They thanked Claire for her time and left. At this point, they were pretty sure they knew their killer.

Roger couldn't wait to tell Donna they can identify her friend's killer. They talked about it all the way back.

When they arrived, both headed straight for Donna and Lou's desks and told them who they found out the killer was.

What happened next shocked everyone present, not just Roger and J.C.!

Both Lou and Donna jumped up from their chairs and yelled at the same time!

*"JASON SULLIVAN?   ARE YOU KIDDING ME?"*

# Chapter 16

The entire floor heard the yelling. Everyone stopped to stare at them. Roger and J.C. were dumbfounded and also stared at their friends. They did not expect this reaction.

Lou said, "I want to see that photo!"

Donna followed, "Me too!"

Roger nodded at J.C. who took off for their desks to pick it up.

Lou took one look and said to Donna, "That's our guy! Look at those beady eyes! That's our guy! Skinny, and ugly!"

Roger replied with, "*Who's* your guy?"

Ignoring the others, Donna stared back at Lou, "That's why he was so nervous! He thought we were there to talk to *him* about Reva!"

"That's why he ducked into the stairway that first day we were there! He probably thought we were looking for him." Lou was staring back at her.

"Hold it! Hold it!" It was Roger, trying to make sense of any of it, let alone all of it. "What are you guys *talking* about? You *know* him?"

"Oh boy, do we…" Donna said more to herself than anyone else. Her mind was spinning a mile a minute.

"Let's all get into an interview room. This is going to take some time to sort out among the four of us." Roger felt like he had been sucker punched.

*What the heck is going on here? They know our killer? How? Why?* Roger's thoughts were crazy, but then again, he figured it might not just be his thoughts at this point. Maybe I need some time off...

They informed Parry they were all going to be in room two. Once settled there, Lou started in with the background they had on Jason.

"He worked part-time for Judge Carrollton, at the courthouse. He ducked away from us the first day we were at the courthouse. I thought that was a bit odd. The next day, we went back to interview people who knew or worked with Judge Gattino and found out he hated Pat. So, we talked to him about her.

"We were thinking, did he hate her enough to kill her? He was very nervous when we first started talking to him, but when we mentioned Pat's name, he settled right down. Donna's right.

He was worried we were going to question him about Reva! However, we had no reason to."

"So you are saying this gal at the dental clinic picked his picture out of one you took at the funeral AND identified him as the man Reva threw out for being drugged up?" Donna was getting over the shock and going into anger.

"Pretty much, yeah." J.C. added, "His mother was also a client, and it seems they have the same address. So Roger and I went out to talk to her. She said Jason left several days ago without telling her where he was going. We checked his room. Almost everything is gone. It doesn't look like he is planning on coming back any time soon."

"Oh, Parry is going to love this. Two murder cases, both killers are known, but we can't find either one of them." Lou could feel his stomach churn.

"Yeah, well, we will get an APB out on Sullivan now. We will put his face out to every law enforcement agency in this country." Roger left the interview room, and J.C. followed.

Donna and Lou stared at each other, then she grabbed her cell.

"Hello? Yes, I need to speak to Judge Carollton, please."

"Hello? Yes. You are his secretary? Fine. This is Detective Donna Decker. I am looking for Jason Sullivan. Is he in?"

"No? When? Okay. Thank you."

Lou jumped in, "Well, what did they say?"

"He hasn't been there in several days and no one knows why. He hasn't called or anything. At this point, the secretary told me, the judge said to inform him he has been 'released' from his position.

"Which, of course, means he has been fired for not showing up. So much for finding him shacked up with a girlfriend or something, after leaving his mother's house."

"Okay, Donna, but you need to let the guys work on their case. We have a missing murderer of our own to catch."

"How right you are. Come on, we have a field trip to make. Before all of this stuff about Jason came up, I made an appointment for us this afternoon. Let's go."

"A field...?" Lou grabbed his jacket since Donna was already halfway to the door.

Once in his car, Lou said, "Okay, fill me in. What direction am I going?"

"We are headed for Derby. You know that 20 acres Jefferson lived on? Well, the new owners tore down the old shack years ago. I guess in the past two or three years, they built a big home in the same place. I want to see if they are aware who owned it before and if they might recognize him if he shows up."

"Good call. By the way, you look awesome today."

"The new owners are Gary and Ann Kastern." Donna smiled at the compliment but didn't acknowledge it.

About a half an hour later, they pulled into a driveway that appeared half a mile long. The house in front of them was a large two-story home. The house and grounds were immaculately taken care of. No doubt the new owners were wealthy.

Lou whistled. It was impressive, all right. Then add a four-car garage to boot.

They rang the doorbell and was greeted by a sixty-ish woman casually dressed who introduced herself as Ann. After introductions to her husband, they were seated in a large family room, overlooking the beautiful view outside.

"Thanks for seeing us on such short notice." Donna smiled, glad to touch base with these people.

The husband, Gary, started, "We don't mind at all, but are a little curious why Wichita's finest would want to see us." His wife, Ann, nodded as she served everyone iced tea.

Donna started with, "Do you know who owned this land before you?"

"Why, no. We bought it out of foreclosure a long time ago. We have no idea who owned it before, but they obviously just walked away. I mean, the little shack that was here was falling down. No one could possibly live in it," Ann said.

Gary finished with, "It went mostly for back taxes, so we really couldn't turn it down all those years ago. We had the shack torn down, then hung onto this acreage for a lot of years until we were ready to build our retirement home.

"When the time came, we cleared the land and built our own home. I have to admit, we really love it here. We found out the original farmhouse was built in the 1800s on the other side of the property, but it burned down about fifty or sixty years ago. I guess that's when the small house was built over here. The highway was on this side of the property by that time, so we figure that's why."

Ann added, "From everything we were able to find out, the original owners were quite wealthy. The farmhouse was large, and they supposedly had all of the amenities for that day."

"The history of old places is awesome, isn't it? Who knows the reasons for things happening so long ago. It is beautiful, though," Donna gave them a big smile.

She hated to drop bad news on them but didn't have a choice. "Here is a picture of the previous owner – the one that lived in the shack. Have you ever seen him before?"

Gary took the prison photo, then passed it on to Ann.

"No. And I don't think I ever want to meet him. He looks pretty scary." Ann was shocked by him.

"I have never seen him either. Why is he in prison?" Gary looked concerned.

Not wanting to go into unneeded detail, Lou said, "He killed someone."

"Ooooh..."

Lou continued, "But he's served his time and has been released. Nothing to worry about, but we would like to touch base with him."

"It is highly unlikely that he would return here, but we wanted you to see his picture, just in case you might see him in the area, or maybe in town." Donna wanted to change the subject before they became too worried.

"Your new home is a far cry from the shack. You made it look like the original high-end home, only modern day!" Donna smiled as the Kasterns both smiled back.

Gary spoke first, "You bet it is. That poor shack was leaning over, ready to fall. We only went through it once, but it was a real mess. Don't know how that man lived in it, even all those years ago. There wasn't even a tornado shelter around here. We had a large 'safe room' built into our basement, so we don't have to worry about it."

Ann explained, "It took 5 months to complete this house. We just kept remembering things we wanted to add to the plans. It was mostly Gary, though..." She smiled at her husband.

"Well, you did it right, I have to tell you. I can see why you are so happy here." Lou really was impressed. Open floor plan, the place had to have two thousand square feet per floor, plus the basement.

They chatted about the weather and how beautiful spring in Kansas was. When offered a chance to be shown a bit of the outside property, they both jumped at it.

"Thank you. We appreciate your taking the time."

The Kasterns were very proud of the place and enjoyed showing Lou and Donna the gardens and three patios behind the house. The swimming pool had water fountains in it which Donna loved. Gary told them the rest of the land was allowed to grow natural like nature wanted it to be.

When they said their goodbyes, they were invited back like they were old friends.

On the way back, Lou and Donna went over the entire pleasant visit repeating some of the funny things the Kastern's said. It isn't often they are on the job and enjoy themselves so much. No, they didn't learn much, but they sure had a good time.

# Chapter 17

J.C.'s mood wasn't any better the following day, but Roger had already mapped out their morning. They were going back and talk with Jason Sullivan's mother, as well as talk to some of the neighbors. They needed all the info on Jason they could get.

When they arrived at Sullivan's house, they were surprised to find no one home. A car was in the drive, but no one answered the door. They knew Claire was disabled and couldn't get around very well, and figured someone must have picked her up to go shopping.

Knocking on neighborhood doors brought up few people who knew them. The lady next door did, however, and was particularly sympathetic.

"Poor dear. Her age and all and have your grown son move in. What a worthless bum. Well, I don't know how she did it. He always wanted something from her. Mostly money. He only worked part-time, you know. It's a blessing he wanted to leave. Good thing he didn't take her car again."

"Take her car? What car?"

"Well, that car is hers you know, the one that's in the driveway. It's not his. Guess she wouldn't let him have it again, 'cause she told me he left without it."

Roger and J.C. thanked the lady and moved on. There was no answer at some of the houses, but the lady across the street was home.

"Well, hello there. I'm Milly. What can I do for you handsome men?" Milly was about sixty. With every hair plastered in place and sporting heavy makeup, she was dressed in a mini-skirt. Flashing long red fingernails and false eyelashes, both men shot their eyebrows up. Roger finally smiled and said they would like to ask her some questions about the lady across the street.

"Come on in, big boy." Milly winked and wiggled herself into the small living room where they all sat down.

"Do you know the lady across the street?"

"Why, yes, I do. She's doesn't keep herself up very well, does she? I have given her the name of my hairstylist and manicurist before, but it didn't do a bit of good." Milly looked crushed.

"Did you know her son, Jason."

"Oh. Him. Only once. I saw him out in the driveway, and I walked over there to introduce myself. You know, just being a friendly neighbor and all. I remember because I was wearing a short summer dress that fit my, uh, figure perfectly. Well, anyway, I told him my name and asked his. Do you know what he did? Why, he told me to mind my own business, that his name was none of my concern!" Her eyebrows raised and she looked horrified.

Roger and J.C. had to struggle to hide the smiles that wanted to appear.

Roger coughed and said, "Have you seen her lately?"

"Yes, of course. She left this morning with some woman I have never seen before. Not that I would know everyone that shows up there, but I have never seen her before. Maybe she is finally going to get her hair done."

"Well, we certainly appreciate your help, M'am. You have been....uh, very helpful." Roger got up to leave.

Milly jumped up and said, "Leaving so soon? You two should stay for lunch. I know it is a bit early, but I am known to be an excellent cook."

It was J.C. who saved the day. "I can certainly believe that, Milly. But our jobs won't allow us to take any more of your time. We do appreciate the offer, though."

Milly smiled and walked with them to the door. She kept waving until they were in their car and drove away.

"So, do you think Milly..."

"Don't! Don't even go there." Roger and J.C. laughed until tears came. Roger was glad to see his partner perk up for a change. The drive back to the station was filled with jokes and laughter.

~~~

Getting back to the squad room, Roger's cell rang just as they were sitting back at their desks. When he got off the phone, there was shock on his face.

"There is another missing woman at the dental clinic."

"Whaaaaa...!" J.C. was already on his feet. Within seconds they were headed back out the door just before noon.

J.C. drove, while Roger repeated the information they were just given.

"Her name is Corey Pattersen. She is nineteen and hasn't worked there more than a couple of months. They gave me all the info they had, including the car she drives. Here is her apartment address. Let's see if her car is there. She isn't answering her cell. Man, we sure don't need any more bodies."

J.C. looked at him and nodded. Roger could see he was worried. He couldn't blame him for being concerned about the dental clinic being a target. This whole thing was crazy.

They drove to the apartment complex where Corey lived. They were able to park near her unit. Her car was not there.

Facing her door, they talked about the possibilities of finding her dead in her car somewhere, like Reva Walters.

"Think we should have a squad check out South Webb, just to make sure...?" J. C. asked.

"Good point, partner. But let's give it a while and see if someone shows up and tries to get into her place." Roger hated just sitting around, but they would need to keep an eye out for anyone trying to enter Corey's apartment.

"Could there really be a psycho targeting their employees? What are the odds, man?"

Roger nodded. "I hear ya."

They continued to exchange thoughts and concerns over this new information. Could Jason Sullivan still be in town? Was he a serial killer or do they have the wrong guy? Could there be two killers? This turn of events had them confused. Time went by slowly, as it usually does on a stakeout.

Not quite two hours later, they were quietly staring at the squirrels running up and down the trees. Suddenly Roger jumped up in his seat and said, "Whoa! Isn't that her car pulling into the parking lot?"

They watched as the car pulled into a parking space close to the missing woman's apartment. There was no movement inside for a couple of minutes. Both Roger and J.C. were holding their breath.

The driver's door opened, and a young woman got out that matched the description of Corey. They jumped out of their vehicle and ran to her.

"Corey? Corey Pattersen?" Roger realized he had been holding his breath.

The young woman swung around, wide-eyed. "Yes...?" She backed up a step as they got closer.

Roger realized she thought they were muggers trying to attack her. He put out his arm to stop J.C., and he stood still. They were about six feet from her.

"Sorry. We didn't mean to scare you. We are detectives from the Wichita Police Department. Here's my badge. You didn't show up for work this morning, and with the fate of Reva Walters, everyone was worried about you. We are just glad to see you are all right."

"Oh, that. Hey, I went to a party last night, and I had too much to drink. I was hung over this morning and didn't want to go in. Surprised they even noticed I was gone. It's a lousy job anyway."

J.C. finally had a chance to take a few deep breaths and became irritated. "You mean to tell me you were hung over and didn't bother to call in sick? You have made a lot of people, myself and my partner included, worry about you, after the horrible death experienced by another employee. What do you have to say for yourself, Corey?"

"I, uh, well... Hey! Back off! I didn't call you, so I am not responsible for your sitting out here. And it's none of your business if I want a day off from a boring job!" Corey huffed and went into her apartment, slamming the door behind her.

Roger and J.C. stared at each other for a moment, then got back into their car. That's when J.C. picked up his cell phone and called the dental clinic.

"Your 'missing' employee, Corey Pattersen, has been found. Yes, I will hold for a moment." He was put on hold for only a few seconds.

"Yes. This is Detective Palmer. Corey Pattersen has been found. She is all right. She was out partying last night, had too much to drink and was hung over this morning. She told us she didn't want to show up at her 'boring job.' Just thought you might want to know." J. C. threw in some sarcasm with the boring job part. "Yeah, sure. Yes, I'll pass that on. Your welcome, Doctor. Yes, goodbye."

"They put Dr. Rong on the phone, and I told him what she said. Well, the good doctor says she doesn't have to be worried about being bored another minute because she doesn't have a job any longer. I like that guy!" He chuckled.

"Boy, what a day. I have to say, I'm relieved she is alright, even if she is an irresponsible twit. And I am glad this day is about over. Let's get back to the precinct." It was only about four o'clock, but Roger was ready to go home. Enough stress for one day.

Back at their desks, J.C. received a call from his wife. After a short conversation, he looked at his partner.

"Come on. We have to go see Parry. Now."

# Chapter 18

"MCGREGOR, DECKER! IN MY OFFICE!"

Total shock hit their faces as they jumped up. It was after four in the afternoon, and they couldn't figure out what the emergency could be. They headed to Parry's office and were surprised to see Roger and J.C. also there. Extra chairs were pushed up for all of them to sit.

Donna looked all around and asked, "Chief, what is it?"

Parry didn't waste any time. "K.T. is missing!"

Lou was the first to speak. "K.T.? Who's K.T.?"

J.C. answered, barely above a whisper, "Karlie, my daughter, is missing. Her mother and I haven't heard from her since the day before yesterday."

"I can sympathize that you haven't heard from her in twenty-four hours, but I guess I do not understand why we were called in here." Lou turned to Roger, whose face showed concern.

"And she is a police officer. Have you checked to see if she has been put on an assignment that kept her out late or something like that?" Donna didn't quite believe a police officer was missing.

"Yes, yes, and yes," Parry said. "We have made all the phone calls and come up empty-handed. She did not have an assignment that would have kept her out last night. All we know at this time is, she received a phone call about four yesterday afternoon and told her supervisor she had to go.

"There was a snitch that said he knew something about the drug case she was working. No one has seen her since. And before you ask, the call came from a burner phone."

Roger and J.C. were quiet. Deadly quiet, as they both looked down at the ground.

"And you want to know why you have been called in here on this new missing person?" Parry looked at them both before continuing.

"Because Erick Jefferson is probably the cause of it."

"Jeffer... Boss, that's insane. Why...?" Lou almost choked the words out.

"Why? Because J.C. was the officer that arrested Erick Jefferson twenty years ago?"

Jaws dropped, Lou and Donna both stared at J.C.

"You… you never told us that." Lou could hardly speak.

"I didn't even know Jefferson was the one hanging these girls until yesterday. Even then, getting revenge with a judge is one thing, but I was just a young patrol officer way back then. I don't get it. Is he going to seek revenge on everyone who has spoken to him?" J.C. was breaking down.

Donna picked up on that. "J.C., I have read that file many times, and your name is not listed as the arresting officer!"

"Fred Perkins was my supervisor at the time. He took credit for everything the 'underlings' did. With Jefferson having a catchy name like 'God's Revenger,' Perkins was interviewed by the press and came out looking like a hero. Everyone loved Perkins. He retired about ten years ago, and I heard he passed away a couple of years after that.

"I didn't mind his taking all the credit. Really. I was just glad Jefferson was off the street." J.C. could hardly speak loud enough to be heard.

Donna could see the wonderful man that Lou had come to admire so much.

It was Parry's turn, "And that is another reason that this looks like Jefferson is involved. Only the killer would know who really arrested him. He knew it was Palmer, not Perkins.

"Roger, you and J.C. head on home. I need to talk to Lou and Donna a little longer. J.C. you stay home tomorrow. Your wife will need you more than we do."

Nodding, they both rose and left the office. Then Parry turned to them.

"Listen, you guys, this has gotten way out of hand. A Deputy Sheriff, a judge, and now a Homicide Detective. We have GOT to stop this man. I know you are doing your best, but that is not good enough.

"Go home and get some rest. Show up tomorrow full of energy and ideas. We have to catch this man before there is another tragedy. Now get out of here."

They quietly left their boss' office.

"Do you really think Karlie is part of our case?"

"Lou, I just don't know. But I am going to take this file home and read it again, and *again* if I have to. There's something we are missing. I can feel it. If Karlie *was* taken by this psycho, she doesn't have long to live."

Back at their desks, Lou got on the phone. Donna kept thinking there was something about Jefferson's file that she was missing. She couldn't remember how many times she had gone through it? But she knew there was *something* she was missing.

So, she grabbed his case file and opened it one more time.

Lou got off the phone with Lucas in Butler County and said there wasn't anything new between them. "Never hurts to check. They did find out the address Jefferson gave was a phony. What a surprise."

Donna told him she was sure there was something they were missing from the file.

Lou yawned and said, "Well, young lady, you just knock yourself out. I would go blind if I had to read it one more time. Speaking of time, isn't it time to go home. I'm starving."

"You are always starving, old man."

"Hey, watch it!"

~~~~~

Donna went home, took a long shower then put on soft, comfy clothes, and made herself a sandwich and some sweet tea. Before eating, she said a prayer thanking God for her food. Then she added, "And God, protect Karlie until we can find her. Please, Lord, don't let her die."

With her meal and drink on the end table next to the couch, she opened the file. She started from page one and read each and every entry carefully. What was she *missing…* and why?

Once again she read how Perkins had arrested him. She wondered how much of the rest of the report was phony. That lousy cop wouldn't get away with that crap today.

Okay, Erick Jefferson was born fifty-five years ago. Since the time he was five, he was raised in this small house on twenty acres outside of Derby. Okay. The land, itself, went for next to nothing. Then his father helped build the house.

His parents died when he was nineteen, but he stayed in the same house he had inherited. That is where he lived when he married. The mortgage on the whole thing was only sixty-five dollars a month. *Wow. Prices were sure cheaper all those years ago!*

His daughter, Dana, was ten when his wife ran off, and he started abusing drugs and booze. Okay.

Dana had to learn how to take care of herself as she grew up. Her best friend, Betsy, was the only good thing in her life. She spent a lot of time with Betsy and her family.

Donna read through dozens of pages, sometimes reading them a second time, trying to see something that she may have missed.

Betsy's parents said they knew Erick had a drinking problem and they suspected drugs. Betsy stayed away from him when she could. The whole family felt sorry for Dana and treated her like their own in order to give her some semblance of a home life.

One Saturday, Betsy didn't come home from the grocery store where she was running an errand for her mom. Her parents waited for a couple of hours before they went looking for her.

The store clerk said she was there and left, so they called the police.

It was the next morning when Betsy's body was found in a ditch south of Wichita, in Sedgwick County. She had been raped multiple times and then strangled to death.

A witness came forward to say he saw Jefferson pick Betsy up at the grocery store. The police went to the country address immediately and arrested Jefferson. He admitted to the crime right away. He said God told him to do it. He had no choice but to do what God told him. Jefferson seemed to think since 'God told him to do it' that he would be set free. That was not the case.

It took a couple of years to go to trial. During his incarceration, Dana hung herself leaving a scathing note about how she hated her father and was afraid if she ever had any children, they would inherit his insanity. The only way to stop it was to kill herself.

Donna put the file down at that point. Some things were too sad to comprehend. She could understand Dana's thinking. Can insanity be inherited? No one knows. Only God. But Donna didn't feel she had to die over it.

Getting up, stretching, and another glass of tea made getting back into reading easier.

Reading the paragraphs on the last pages… nothing. Donna was frustrated. She would have to start over.

Page one… Fred Perkins was the arresting officer…

And on it went. This time she took each page out by itself, forcing herself to pay particular attention to it.

After going through each page again, Donna still couldn't find what she was looking for. It was almost midnight when she closed it down and went to bed.

Sleep is what she needed now. Lots of sleep, and it didn't take her long to find it.

# Chapter 19

When Donna's alarm went off at six the following morning, she didn't want to get up. Having dreams throughout the night robbed her of the rest she so desperately needed.

It was apparent the flurry of thoughts in her sleep was about the info she had devoured the night before. She poured her first cup of coffee, then noticed the case folder lying on the table.

Donna turned away from the file, and started to sip the hot coffee, when the shock hit her!

She dropped her cup, and didn't even notice as it shattered on the floor sending coffee everywhere!

"No! It *can't* be! Yes, it *can!*" She *knew!* Donna *knew* where to find Karlie!

She grabbed her cell and called Lou. She told him to come pick her up fast. Donna then called Parry at home to tell him she knew where Karlie was!

"I don't have time to explain, but I need a SWAT team to meet Lou and I at the QuickTrip on south Rock Road and E. Patriot St.

"Tell them to come prepared for trouble!" She hung up when he agreed.

Donna quickly brushed her teeth, got dressed making sure she had her gun and holster ready.

She went outside as Lou was pulling up to her house.

"What in the world is going on, woman! I was…"

"I think I know where Jefferson is holding Karlie!"

"You whaaaa…Where am I headed?"

"We are meeting a SWAT team. at the QuickTrip on south Rock, close to Derby. Move it!"

Heading south, it took less than ten minutes to reach their destination. It was another five before six heavily armed officers pulled up in a bullet-proof van.

The detectives pulled their Captain, Slade Baker, over to Lou's car. Donna pulled a county map from her purse and spread it out on the front hood.

As fast as she could, she explained her plan.

"Look, guys, I know we don't know exactly where we're going, but we will have to improvise. Jefferson was a small boy when his parents bought that land out in the country and built that small house. They died when he was nineteen, and he stayed on, paying the small mortgage payments."

"Yeah, but he lost that back to the bank after he was arrested!"

"Yes, Lou, you and I know that, but that is the only place he has ever known – except prison. Where else would he go?

"Now, remember what Ann said about the old shack – that there wasn't even a tornado shelter there? Well, the original house on the other side of the property *would* have had one.

"No one could live in this part of the mid-west without a tornado shelter! Plus, back in the 1800s, they would have also needed a food cellar. They were one and the same. Erick knew that and used *that* shelter whenever lousy weather struck, so he didn't need one next to his small house.

"I believe that's where he has Karlie. There is an underground shelter somewhere on the back side of this property. And if the original house is any indication, it will be a large shelter. The owners were wealthy in their day. We just have to find it!"

Lou was shocked. "You are amazing! And *right!* Good Lord!"

Slade was more conservative. "Nice going, detective. We have to find this place while being completely quiet, so he doesn't hear us. Let's go over that map again."

They spent a few more minutes discussing where to go and how to get there. Slade then left with his team, and they followed.

Finding the back side of the property off a dirt road, they all parked and climbed over a barbed wire fence. Each person was given a hand-held clicker, made initially for dog training, but worked perfectly for the team when silence was needed.

As they spread out, the first person to find an entrance going underground was to click once – only once, so Erick would not be alarmed if he heard it. The officer would then hold up his hand so everyone could see and join him, before entering.

What seemed longer under stress, was only minutes. Lou, Donna, and the SWAT team were on high alert. As the new owners had stated, the majority of the acreage was left to grow naturally. They walked through tall grass, trees and over a small creek. About eleven minutes out, a click was heard.

Donna was sure she stopped breathing. Had they found it? They quietly moved in the direction of the officer standing perfectly still with his arm straight up. Within a minute, everyone was looking at the same thing. A small hill was covered by tall grass all around. And there was a door in the middle that appeared to lead underground.

Slade moved Lou and Donna back. His men had on helmets and were dressed in bulletproof vests. They weren't so the SWAT team would go in first. Everyone had their guns drawn.

After carefully opening the door, they could see the steps leading down. There seemed to be no end to them without turning flashlights on, but that was not possible at this time. If Jefferson was down there, he would see the light.

Three men started down the stairs. Slowly. Quietly. When they reached the last step, they could barely see but was aware they were in a large room. A light was coming from under the door of a room on the other side. While two waited perfectly still, the third quietly walked back up the stairs and told the others.

Without a sound, they all entered and met at the bottom of the stairs. They made their way to the entrance of the lighted room. Lou and Donna followed behind as they were told to do.

They stood in front of the door for a couple of minutes. No sound came from the inner room. Donna was sure she wasn't breathing.

With a nod from Slade, one of the men rammed the door, and it flew open. The team ran into the room.

"STAND WHERE YOU ARE!"

"DON'T MOVE!"

"DOWN ON YOUR KNEES!"

When Lou and Donna obtained entry, they could see the team had Erick Jefferson at gunpoint. He was down on his knees with his hands high in the air.

Donna rushed over to the side of the room where she found Karlie naked, sitting on the floor with her hands tied above her head. She was unconscious and not moving. Next to her was a makeshift bed. Donna grabbed the blanket and covered her.

Not sure if she was still alive, she kept talking to her. "Karlie? We're here, honey. You are safe. You're safe now."

Finally, Karlie opened her eyes and gave a small smile. Donna thought she would cry right in front of everyone.

Donna yelled, "She's alive!" Everyone cheered!

That is when Erick made his move. With one second of their attention taken away from him, he made a jump for his gun. Just as he swung it around, a bullet went between his eyes, followed by five more to the chest.

He stood there for a moment as if trying to figure out what to do next, then slowly slid to the floor.

The SWAT team wasn't finished. They checked every inch of the shelter to make sure there wasn't more rooms or another perp.

Within minutes, the place was secure. Slade had called it in while Lou and Donna cared for Karlie.

She insisted on standing up. Karlie secured the blanket around her so she could walk over to Jefferson's body.

The SWAT Team parted and let her in. She stared down at the man who had raped and terrorized her for almost two days. He had a plain heart tattoo outlined on his left arm, with the name Dana inside.

Donna could not imagine what was going through her mind. Her clothes were found neatly folded, so Donna helped her get dressed while Lou held the blanket up, like a privacy wall. An ambulance took her away shortly afterward.

It took two hours more for CSI to comb the underground rooms for further evidence. It was apparent Erick Jefferson had been living there since his release from prison.

They found his small blue Ford parked close by, covered in grass and tree limbs. It could not have been seen even by helicopter. Seems Jefferson had thought of everything.

Lou and Donna stayed behind to get a good look at the underground cavern. It was even more significant than Donna could have imagined. They found tunneling that went to the original farmhouse that was no longer there. Following it, Donna pushed open a small door that went up to the sunlight. She looked around, trying to envision the original home, with its ingenious escape route – whether for safety from severe weather or something more sinister.

Before leaving the property, they went to the other side to see Gary and Ann.

"Hi, there! How nice to see you again! What brings you way out here?" Gary was all smiles.

After getting Gary and Ann sitting in their den, Lou explained the entire morning's events to them. They were shocked, but relieved things turned out for the good.

"You can bet I will be getting rid of that storm shelter! I would have nightmares just thinking about what – or who – could be hiding there!"

"It is currently a crime scene, so wait until the authorities are through with it, then do whatever you feel like. I have to say, I would get rid of it too if I were you!" Donna let out a chuckle but was very serious.

It had been an exhausting day already, and it was only eleven in the morning. Lou and Donna grabbed something to eat before heading back to the precinct.

When they walked in, everyone there stood and applauded. Parry even came out of his office and joined in. They were thrilled at the outcome of this case, but with it over, the mental exhaustion had come rushing in.

"You guys come into my office." Parry was smiling.

After the door was shut, he said, "Nice job, guys. I can't say it any other way. Donna, it was quite an inspiration you had, and it paid off. Nice work."

Donna blushed but didn't say a word.

"You have worked a lot on this case, and it is time you had a day off. Don't come in tomorrow. And if you need another day off, don't come in the next day. And if you want another day off, TOO BAD! you have to come back to work THEN!"

Lou and Donna burst out laughing and started teasing him.

" Aw, man! You're so cruel!"

"Too bad. You don't get it. Now get out of here. Write up your reports and go home. I don't want to see you here tomorrow."

They spent two hours wrapping up their case, making sure every moment was in writing, interspersed with congratulations coming from fellow detectives.

On their way out the door, Donna whispered to Lou, "I don't know about you, but the best part of my day was seeing that bullet between Jefferson's eyes. And I won't apologize for it."

Lou laughed. "It was indeed a pretty sight."

# Chapter
# 20

Roger showed up at the hospital early the next morning. He found Karlie and her parents there.

"Hi there, Uncle Detective!" Karlie seemed to be in high spirits. She always called him uncle due to his closeness with her parents.

"Hi there, yourself. I stopped by to see what your excuse was for not being at work *again* today! However, I see you just want to lounge around. J.C. you need to talk to this girl. She is never going to make detective if all she wants to do is take naps!"

J.C. followed the joke, "What can I do? I've tried to tell her, but you know kids! They just don't listen!."

All four of them laughed. Roger gave her a hug and told her how proud he was of her for making it through such a tough time.

"You will be the one I think of the next time I get myself in a jam. If I can make it through like you, I will be just fine."

Everyone was teary-eyed. Then Karlie changed the tone.

"Ah, you're just jealous cause I get to sleep in and you don't."

"Oooooh! Busted!" J.C. pointed at his partner.

Laughter rang again. It lasted so long a nurse looked in and asked if everything was all right, causing the merriment to continue.

J.C. finally told his wife and daughter goodbye. It was time for him and Roger to get to work. He kissed his daughter on the forehead.

"I love you." He then left with his partner.

Karlie was getting released later today and was going to spend the next couple of days at home with her parents. She was on indefinite leave from work but insisted she would be back to work on Monday morning.

~~~

It was sleep Donna needed most to rid her mind of the past twenty-four hours. Having the day off, Donna slept in until nine. When she had returned home the night before, she cleaned up the broken cup and spilled coffee, but after a long shower, she fell fast asleep.

The next morning, she was enjoying a cup of coffee in her pajamas when she called the hospital and talked with Karlie. Donna was so glad to hear her happy voice.

Karlie thanked Donna for saving her life and said she was so grateful. Things couldn't have turned out any better. *By Your Grace, Almighty God, Karlie was not a statistic. Thank you, Lord.*

About eleven, Lou called and said he wanted to talk to her about something. They agreed to meet at his house about one o'clock.

When she arrived, Lou had a pitcher of sweet tea and snacks out in the family room where they got comfortable. He didn't have a pool in the backyard like his mother did, but the view from the glass wall was beautiful. Soft music made it a pleasant place to relax.

Donna snuggled up to a pillow at the end of the couch while Lou was sitting in the chair next to her.

For over an hour they talked about friends and family. They never had a problem chatting. Donna was so happy to be with Lou and not on the job. Never once was the case mentioned, other than the calls each had made to Karlie that morning.

"Okay, hot stuff, what did you want to talk to me about?" Donna grinned.

Lou gave a big smile and said, "You think I'm hot stuff? Really?" They both laughed.

When things got quiet again, Lou started slowly…

"I have to talk to you about something. You may not like it, but I can no longer keep it to myself. Something has to give."

That worried Donna, and she sat up straight. "What is it, Lou? Is it your mom?" Was Darlene ill, or dying? Was he? Her mind raced while her heart stopped.

"No. It's you."

"It's *me*…?"

"Yes, darn it, Donna. I am in love with you, and I can't hold it in any longer. There, it's out. I said it. I am glad it's done.

"Now don't say a word. Just hear me out. I didn't want this to happen. It's not like I made it happen. I fought it as long as I could. I just fell madly and completely in love with you. I have wanted to tell you for a long time."

Lou stood in front of her, "I know you must hate me for this, but…

Donna stood up and kissed him on the mouth. "You talk too much."

"I do?" Lou was stunned at what just happened.

"Sit beside me, Lou."

Holding both his hands, she knew it was her time. "Lou, I am in love with you, too."

Lou's eyes got big, but he seemed unable to move. "How long has this been going on? How long have you let me suffer thinking you would hate me for falling for you! You love me? Do you really?"

"I have been against telling you because of what it will do to our careers. You know it will end us being partners, and I don't think I could stand that. Working with you every day has made the job so wonderful. It would not be the same without you. I mean, I love my job, but I love you more."

"I know that feeling." He leaned over and gave Donna a soft kiss on the lips. She was pretty sure she melted. His kiss was just as she always imagined it would be.

Lou spoke up, "I have given this a lot of thought, and I may have an answer for us. So hear me out before you say no."

Lou told her what he thought their options were. They talked about each one in depth.

Hours went by as they formulated a plan. They both knew they wanted to be together and together they would be. They finally figured out what they were going to do.

When evening came, neither was hungry. They just wanted to hold each other tight.

The next morning found Donna lying in Lou's bed with his arms around her. She didn't think she had ever been so happy. Seems they would take that second day off, after all.

~~~

The rapes had caused Karlie pains and minor bruising, but she was going to be all right. Erick Jefferson was careful not to create bruising that would call into doubt that her hanging was a suicide.

Karlie explained to her parents she would not let that "perp" ruin her life. She made it clear she still wanted to be a detective like J.C.

What she went through pained her father. But he was so grateful she was alive, that the thought of her being an officer on the streets again wasn't even an issue.

J.C. now wanted to get their own case wrapped up. There was still a murderer loose, and he didn't want some other parent to go through what he almost had to go through. It was terrible enough Reva Walter's family had to suffer.

The first step was to go back to Claire Sullivan's house. They needed to ask her some more questions.

Driving out to the southeast side of town for the partners was like old times. Both were in great moods and joked about everything. Seems the stress of the past few days was completely gone.

That is until they pulled up in front of Claire's house. There was a For Sale sign in the yard, and the house was empty. The car was gone as well.

They walked around the house and looked over the back fence. All the patio furniture was also gone.

J.C. ran for Milly's house to find out what she knew, while Roger sat back down in the car and wrote down the name and number of the real estate agent listing the home.

*Where could she have gone?*

"It's not like she had a bunch of money or anything!" Roger knew he was talking to himself. "Where could she have gone? Jason was her only son, and he ran off. There's no one else that we know of..."

Roger jumped into the car. "Milly said a box truck pulled up here yesterday and emptied the house out completely. It said Goodwill on the side of it. The vehicle was driven off at the same time the truck left.

"She hasn't seen anyone near the house except the real estate agent who walked through the house, put the sign in the yard and drove off."

Roger called the real estate company and asked for the agent. He was told the agent went out of town but would be back in two days.

"If you are interested in seeing one of her home listings, one of the other agents could show it for her." The secretary was sweet, but that seemed to irritate him.

Roger identified himself and told her he wanted to know about the owner of a listing.

"Well, we don't have that information. The listing agent is the only one who has had contact with the owners. Sorry."

He hung up and told J.C. they were going to have to wait two days for any more information.

~~~

Lou and Donna's time off was over. However, it was the most important time they have ever had. They believed their future was planned.

At the precinct, they were again congratulated on bringing down a killer. A small crowd was at their desks. Donna told them it was the SWAT team, not them, that brought the bad guy to his fate.

That is when Lou jumped in, "Yeah, sure, but we would not have been able to rescue Karlie at all if you hadn't figured out where she was being held. That was ingenious, girl! You need to explain to us how you came up with it."

Donna thought for a moment. "Well, as you know, I re-read that file a couple more times. But this time, my reading the information was accompanied by the additional pieces we had gathered from the new owners, Gary and Ann. That's what completely changed things.

"I mean, they said he didn't have a tornado shelter. But he had lived there almost all of his life. There had to be one. And if there was one, it was one that no one knew about but him. A perfect hiding place.

"It only figured the shelter had to be where the *original* big house was since the little house didn't have one.

"When the weather got bad, they would run for the big underground shelter. End of story."

# Chapter 21

Lou and Donna requested a meeting with Parry on the morning they returned.

While that meeting was taking place, Roger received a phone call. It was from Claire Sullivan.

"Claire! Where are you? We have been worried about you?"

"Thank you, detective, but there's no need to worry about me."

"We need to talk to you, Claire. Can you come in?"

"I need to talk to you, too. I am afraid I am unable to come to you, but you can certainly visit me." She gave him the address, and Roger said they would be there in thirty minutes.

Roger and his partner were excited to be able to ask more questions and maybe get some much-needed answers. They were shocked when they pulled up in front of an upper-middle-class home on a lovely street in east Wichita.

"How did she get *here?*" Roger wasn't entirely putting things together yet.

Roger rang the doorbell, and a nurse came to the door. They identified themselves and were let in. The detectives were then taken to a bedroom where they were shown Claire lying in bed. The nurse shut the door on her way out.

"What is going on here, Claire?" J.C. was just as confused as Roger.

"Gentlemen, please sit down. I get tired easy, so forgive me for getting right to the point. You are going to have to hear my story from the beginning, so please be patient."

They pulled up two chairs next to the bed and sat down. Roger held her hand as she talked.

"My husband died when my son, Jason, was only nine years old. It was tough on a small child like that, I know. I did everything I could think of to make his life seem normal, but he would have none of it. By the time he was a teen, he was out of control and totally living in a world that only had room for him.

"All Jason ever wanted from me was money. My love never mattered. It was as though he didn't even know what the word meant. He certainly never showed me any. I didn't have much money. Oh, I wasn't destitute or anything as I was very frugal about saving every dime I could after my husband died.

"His life insurance paid off my mortgage and put some money in the bank. I did my best to live on my disability, so I wouldn't use up my savings. However, that money couldn't go on forever. Jason knew about the money and would try all kinds of things to get it for himself.

"Anyway, you are looking for him because he killed that Reva woman, aren't you?

Roger and J.C. were shocked at her statement and just stared at her.

"I know you are, I know... You don't have to say a word. Let me tell you how I know.

"One night he came home covered in blood. Thinking it was his, I was horrified and asked him what happened. Well, he told me he got stoned and 'went after that woman' who threw him out of the dental office. I knew about it the day it happened. He came home furious.

"He just couldn't forgive her for the public humiliation. I can't understand what he thought would happen. You just don't get stoned out of your mind and impose that on people. I would have done the same thing she did, poor woman.

"So I asked, what do you mean you went after her? He said he attacked her in her car and killed her. That is where all the blood came from. He talked about it like it was an ordinary everyday event. I have to tell you, I was about to lose it!

"The person I was looking at was suddenly a stranger. I didn't recognize him at all. He murdered someone! Who was this evil scumbag? Jason then said he needed to get out of town and wanted me to give him 'the money in the bank' to live on! Can you believe that? It was MY money in the bank, not his! He thought I would just give it to him so he could get away with murder.

"I was stunned. He just stated he had killed someone and then said he wants me to give him all my money to help him get away and live elsewhere. What was I supposed to live on while he was spending my money?

"That's when it happened, gentlemen. That is when it happened. I hit a wall. One I should have hit years ago.

"I told him to go shower and throw away any clothes with blood on it. I further said for him to pack up everything he owned into black plastic bags because we didn't have suitcases.

"The first thing in the morning, I said, I would go to the bank and get him the money he needed. Jason wanted it that night so he could leave right then, but I told him I would only be able to get a small amount out from an ATM machine so he would have to wait until morning. He had no choice but to agree.

"I then told him I was going to fix us an excellent dinner – since it would probably be the last one we would ever have together. I would do that while he cleaned up.

"Well, Jason headed for the bathroom to take a shower. After he got out, he piled everything he wanted into three black plastic bags, which was piled by the front door for easy access to my car.

"You see, detectives, he didn't care about me. He didn't care it would be our last meal together. He didn't care about what I was supposed to live on when he took all of my money. He didn't care that the car he was going to take was mine! You see, Jason didn't care about anyone but himself.

"But, he's my son, so I made a nice dinner, and we sat and talked at the table. At least I spoke to him. He didn't have much to say.

"I told you earlier that I had hit a wall? For the first time, or at least that I will admit to, I saw the rotten pile of flesh in front of me for what he was. A drugged-out murderer and a self-centered, thieving, con man.

"Well, he was just about finished with our wonderful dinner when he starting foaming at the mouth and fell over dead. Oh, did I mention I poisoned him? Yeah. Well, he's the one that pushed me into that wall. I figured I brought him into this world, I could surely take him out. And so I did. I am just sorry I didn't think of it before that woman was killed.

"Oh, I see your faces. You are in shock, aren't you? Well, how do you think he left town? On foot? The car was still there. I can no longer drive, so it wasn't much use to me.

"Before you ask a bunch of questions, let me finish before I get too tired. Okay, so he's dead. Good riddance. I was surprised at how little emotions I felt about it. My backyard was having a patio poured in two days. I was having that done to help with the resale of the house since I knew I was not going to be able to stay there much longer.

"They had dug out the dirt and put in the frame stuff. They were ready to pour cement in a couple of days. Well, I have to admit, it wasn't easy, but I spent several hours outside in the dark, digging up a hole big enough for Jason under the one already there. I am sure it is the only time I was glad he was short and skinny.

"I had to do it in the dark because I couldn't risk a neighbor seeing me. Well, after I got it down about four feet – yep, I dug that far down. I drug Jason's body out the door, over the hole and dropped him in it. He fit like a charm, but then I had to start shoveling dirt back in.

"Before you start asking silly questions, please don't think I am completely stupid. I know the dirt has to be stamped down firmly for the cement to be poured. I was raised by a construction worker.

"Had I been male, that probably would have been my profession, too. Oh, I know women can do that today, but back in my time, a woman would have been laughed right out the door. Too bad, really.

"Anyway, I didn't want the company coming two days later to think it had been tampered with, so every shovel or two, I would spend time stamping it down as far as it would go. All around his body, making sure every crevice was filled and stable. Like I said, it took hours.

"I hurt pretty bad by the time I finished, but I admit, it looked great. If I hadn't known any better, I would have sworn it hadn't been touched.

"The following morning, I called Goodwill and told them I had a ton of clothes, video games and other small items they could have. They added me to their rounds that day and picked up the black plastic bags that had all of his stuff in them. I even threw in some things I no longer wanted as well as a couple small furniture pieces. My house never looked so good!

"I spent more time in the backyard that day, too. I watered the dirt to help it settle some more. Added more soil.... sigh... It was quite the job. Hard to do when you have a bum leg that doesn't want to cooperate. But, the next day when they came to pour the cement, there wasn't any sign of him left. They leveled out some gravel, then poured the cement.

"And I have to admit, that patio was awesome. Wish I had done it years ago when I could have enjoyed it myself.

"If you two are wondering how I felt about killing my own son, I have to be honest. I felt nothing. He was more a dangerous animal than human. All I needed to do was put him down.

"So, gentlemen, I truly appreciate you not interrupting me while I got through my story.

"Now for the last chapter. I am dying. I have been for the previous six months actually, that I know of. I even told my son, but he didn't care. He wanted to make sure I left a will leaving every dime to him. I told him I had. It wasn't true, but I said it was.

"I have left everything to Goodwill. What little I have. The money from the sale of my house will go to pay for my costly stay here in hospice." Claire took a deep breath and sighed.

"Hospice? I was afraid of that." It was Roger who finally found his voice. He had heard about several lovely homes in Wichita being renovated to take care of dying people. This attractive ranch-style home appeared to be a four bedroom, but he noticed coming in the front door, a hall opening to the garage that had been made into two more bedrooms. It now made sense.

"I am exhausted, so if you have any questions, ask me now, or you may never get any answers."

"I...uh..." J.C. couldn't even get the words out.

"I know you will want to arrest me for the murder of my son, but I am afraid I will not live long enough for you to prosecute. I am here because I have advanced stage four cancer and have only about a week to live... maybe only days. It wasn't easy, but I have come to terms with it.

"Do you think my son cared? Never blinked an eye when I told him. Not once did he ever say, 'I am sorry you're dying, Mom?' Not once."

Roger got up and spoke slowly. "I am so sorry about your cancer, Claire. Thank you for telling us what happened. We really do appreciate it. We are going to let you rest now. If you need anything, anything at all, please call us. Promise me you will."

Claire smiled and nodded.

The two detectives walked out in silence. The nurse let them out and locked the door behind them. When they were back in the car, both sat staring out the window for several minutes.

"Could this get more *unbelievable*?"

"No."

"Is any of this real?"

"No."

"Have we gone crazy?"

"Yes."

"Do we have to tell Parry?"

"Yes."

Roger started the car and drove them back to the precinct in silence, each buried in their own thoughts.

# Chapter
# 22

It was early morning over a week later when Donna stepped up to Reva's grave. She put the handful of bright pink Bleeding Hearts flowers in the vase in front of her stone. Those flowers were one of her friend's favorites, so Donna knew she would like them.

"They got him, Reva. They got the man who did this to you. I would like to say it was my doing, but it wasn't. I wanted to be the one to bring him to justice, but it looks like his mother beat me to it. Can you believe that, girl? His mother revenged you. Oh, I don't think that was her main reason, but she accomplished it anyway."

Donna stayed a few more minutes to talk with her friend, then left to go to work. She wanted to hug the two detectives who worked so hard to crack this case.

"Thank you, again." Donna was looking at Roger.

"I would like to take credit for bringing this sleazeball to justice, but I am afraid his mother did that." Roger chuckled.

"I never met her," Donna replied, "but I really like her." Roger chuckled again.

"She was a nice lady. Claire passed away two days ago. J.C. and I stopped by one more time to say goodbye. Of course, our case is closed. Is everything ready here?" Roger smiled at his friend.

"Yes," Donna said. "All we have to do is wait for Parry to show up."

Everyone was a bit nervous. Parry had been called down to the D.A.'s office for a meeting. It had been prearranged so they could get ready for their boss' surprise birthday party.

Folding tables with food all over them were in the middle of the room. A few wrapped packages sat on the end. They were as ready as they were ever going to be.

Donna's cell rang, and she jumped on it. It was the DA warning her Parry was on his way back.

"Quiet everyone! He's on his way now. He will be getting off the elevator any minute!"

Just then, the elevator bell gave it's notorious "ding," and the door opened.

"SURPRISE!"

"HAPPY BIRTHDAY!"

Stepping through the opening doors, Parry was so shocked he couldn't talk.

'This is a first! The boss is without words!" The whole room laughed.

"What is going on here? I take it you guys don't have any work to do. Should have told me and I would have given you some." Parry sounded gruff but had a smile on his face.

They had a great time teasing him about being old at fifty-nine.

"Time to get out the rocking chair!"

"Rocking chair? That takes energy, and he doesn't have any left!"

Everyone snacked on the food and drinks while patting Parry on the back for making it so long. It was soon time for him to open his 'presents.'

The first one was an adult diaper – fit for an elderly man. Everyone laughed till tears appeared. Parry took it in good stride and put it on over his slacks. Everyone got out their phones for a picture.

The next package opened was a navy blue t-shirt. In large white letters, it said "I am not 59. I am 18 with 41 years experience!"

More laughter while he pulled it on over his shirt. Between the funny t-shirt and the huge diaper, it was a great time.

Another package was long and round. It was a cane which he started using.

The last gag gift was a yellow metal sign for his office. "WAIT! I AM HAVING A SENIOR MOMENT."

When the phones rang, someone always ran to take care of it. Luckily, nothing serious occurred.

The D.A. showed up a few minutes later and howled at Parry in his diaper, t-shirt, and cane.

Everyone loved the memories that would last forever.

As the day was wearing on, Lou stepped in front of everyone.

"Hey, guys! Can I have your attention? I have some news to pass on that you may – or may not – want to hear!"

The group got quiet and turned their attention to him.

"Donna, come join me."

Donna and Lou put their arms around each other, and the wolf whistles started.

Lou motioned them to stop. "Yeah, I can see the envy on all your faces, but you can't have her. She's mine!"

"Now before you all pass out. I want to announce Donna and I will be leaving the force at the end of this day. We gave our notice well over a week ago to our Birthday Boy, here.

"See, the problem is, we have fallen in love – with each *other*, no less - and want to be together. She and I will be married in three weeks – and you are all invited – at Roger Duncan's house.

"After our honeymoon – no, I am not going to tell you where we are going – we will be opening up our own private detective agency, right here in Wichita. That way we can do what we love doing and still work together."

Cheers and applause followed his remarks. Lou leaned down and kissed her on the mouth. The crowd started the cheering again.

"Okay, okay. Quiet. We wanted you to know if you ever need anything from us, we will be there for you. Just give us a call. You will find us in the phone book under McGregor Investigations, Inc."

The final hour had people talking in several groups while others congratulated Lou and Donna. Birthday wishes were being repeated to Parry as people prepared to leave for the day.

When second shift started arriving, Lou and Donna helped Parry clean up the food tables while filling the refrigerator in the break room. The birthday boy had removed his diaper and t-shirt before second-shift started to arrive. He felt that would be too much for them to handle.

In the break room, it was Parry's turn.

"I know you guys were the instigators in this party. I thank you. As crazy as my people are, I love them all. And I want you to know, you will be missed around here." He gave each of them a hug.

"Our pleasure, boss. And you will be sorely missed as well." Lou was near tears as the realization soaked in he would never be a part of this wonderful group of people again.

"We won't be far away, always remember that." Donna gave him a kiss on the cheek. Then they said their goodbyes.

# UNHOLY REVENGE

~~~~~~~~~~~~~~~~~~

# Epilogue

Lou and Donna were married three weeks later. Her smiling father gave her away while her mother cried happy tears on the front row. They were so thrilled to see their darling daughter finally in love. Lou's mother, however, could only talk about grandchildren. She would settle for six… maybe.

The happy couple took two weeks to spend time in Hawaii, running the beaches, dining out and staring into each other's eyes.

Selling her townhouse, Donna McGregor moved into her new husband's lovely home. He gave her cart blanc to decorate or change anything she desired. She did make some changes, mostly in the master bedroom so it would be more inviting for the two of them.

They purchased a building on an acre lot on the north side of Wichita for their business. It took about three months to get everything up and running, but it was worth the effort. A secretary was hired to run the front office and keep track of appointments.

Almost immediately, the phone started to ring. If you were going to hire a detective, it was obvious people wanted those who have had experience. These were not newbies. They knew the law and what they could do to get the information needed in each case.

Lou and Donna were so happy being together and having a new business, they couldn't see how anything could be any better.

Then, Donna discovered she was pregnant with a baby girl.

They named her Reva Jane.

~~~~~~~~~~~~~~~~~~~~~

# Thank You!

Thank you for reading UNHOLY REVENGE. I hope you enjoyed it as much as I did writing the story.

I would appreciate it if you would leave a review.

If this is the ebook, just click here http://bit.ly/DB_books and pick this book to review.

Otherwise, go to Amazon.com and type in this book name. It will only take a moment of your time and it means so much to an author to hear from her readers.

God Bless,
Donalie Beltran